"You'll have to be nice to me, won't you, Jemma?"

Jemma paled, unable to put her fears into words. He was making her feel like a poor relation, begging for a crust! And what did he mean by nice?

"You're not going to..." she gulped. The fever climbed within her.

"Surely you didn't think I was helping you without expecting something in return?" he murmured softly, his eyes lingering on her mouth, then dropping to her breasts.

He was deliberately building sexual tension, Jemma thought angrily. What did she have to give him but her body? "I said I'd do this job if you didn't touch me!"

"I remember," the Count said silkily, "but I can't recall that I agreed to your terms."

SARA WOOD lives in a rambling sixteenth-century home in the medieval town of Lewes amid the Sussex hills. Her sons have claimed the cellar for bikes, making ferret cages, taxidermy and winemaking, while Sara has virtually taken over the study with her reference books, word processor and what have you. Her amiable, tolerant husband, she says, squeezes in wherever he finds room. After having tried many careers—secretary, guest house proprietor, play group owner and primary teacher—she now finds writing romance novels gives her enormous pleasure.

Books by Sara Wood

SARA WOOD

the count's vendetta

Harlequin Books

TORONTO • NEW YORK • LONDON
AMSTERDAM • PARIS • SYDNEY • HAMBURG
STOCKHOLM • ATHENS • TOKYO • MILAN

Harlequin Presents first edition April 1989
ISBN 0-373-11166-5

Original hardcover edition published in 1988
by Mills & Boon Limited

CHAPTER ONE

THE blood-red Ferrari growled throatily as it slid into the car park, its sleek, ostentatious lines a magnet for everyone's eyes. Its arrival made Jemma Mortimer's pulses quicken, and alerted her dulled brain.

Up to that moment, she'd been expecting to cope with the day reasonably well. It would be gruelling, she knew that, but since her mother's death she'd found it easier to conceal her own feelings and not give in to stress. It meant less worry for her father. But the sight of that wretched flamboyant Italian car shattered her composure, shredding it and flinging it into the spring breeze.

It had never occurred to her that Count Vasari would deign to turn up. Colour drained slowly from her face, and she steadied herself against the porch as strength ebbed from her body. He mustn't see her weakness. With a supreme effort, Jemma summoned up enough of her formidable will-power to prevent the sick anger from destroying her image.

It must be someone else, she told herself fiercely, some other rich extrovert with a taste for power and opulence. She stared down at her smart black stiletto shoes, the same refrain going round and round in her head. It wasn't him, it couldn't be him—not after all the years he'd ignored them, his haughty, heartless silence reaching out across the miles like icy fingers to permeate their lives!

From under her lashes she saw the handmade, glove-soft shoes hit the ground, saw the long, muscular, black-clad legs. Heaven help her, it *was* Vasari! Her mind racing wildly, she turned her head away before he could see her. There was something almost superstitious about her determination to avoid publicly acknowledging his presence, as though that would give him the advantage. Whatever happened, she wouldn't look up and meet his eyes, for almost certainly she'd experience once again what it was to feel terrible, destructive heartache. Today she had enough sorrow without putting herself through the wringer on his account.

A car door slammed, gravel crunched and a murmur ran through the people around her. Jemma's pale, glossed lips twisted. Until he died, that man would make heads turn and people whisper. With a harsh intake of breath, she spun on her heel and walked shakily into the church, blocking out everything except putting one foot in front of the other and making it to the front pew before she forgot herself and allowed her shock to become a talking point.

Charles and Christobel, her neighbours and closest friends, had followed her down the aisle. They slipped in beside her and looked anxiously at the pure profile of the beautiful woman who stared so rigidly ahead.

'Are you all right?' asked Christobel, placing a friendly hand on her arm. 'Would you like Charles to get you a glass of water?'

Jemma lifted her chin proudly, struggling against emotion. She had a lot to get through today, and somehow she must deal with Vasari too. Fate was twisting the knife, and no mistake. He'd done this on purpose, she thought savagely; it was just like a man with his vicious, twisted mind to sweep in, surrounded by a panoply of wealth, and give her an inferiority complex again. Memories flashed cruelly through her brain, tormenting her with moments of happiness that she would prefer to remain buried for ever.

'Jemma?'

Christobel was shaking her gently. Jemma smoothed out her face and deliberately hardened her eyes.

'I'm all right. Just don't let that evil Italian anywhere near me,' she said tightly. 'I might do something unexpected, like tear his hair out at the roots.'

Christobel exchanged an astonished glance with her husband. The idea of the cool and elegant Jemma acting so uncharacteristically was startling. Yet they'd heard about the cruel vendetta against her family, and presumably this was its haughty instigator. 'You don't mean that's . . .'

'Please!' Jemma's voice sounded strained. 'I don't want to talk about it. As far as I'm concerned, the less I discuss it, the better.'

The vicar, a little disconcerted that the principal mourner had gone ahead of the procession, entered the church. Slowly Jemma rose, clutching at the polished top of the pew for support. Her brother's coffin passed, followed by Luisa's.

She could manage, as she had planned. All it needed was the will-power to wipe Vasari out of her mind. Jemma held her slender body erect, the delicate bones of her face touchingly ethereal beneath the elegant black toque and veil. Her ash-blonde hair had, as usual, been swept into its smoothly coiled chignon, exposing a vulnerable length of neck. But anyone looking at her would also see the strength and determination in the

stance of her body and the set of her mouth. She was a
contradiction: a fragile woman with a steel core.

Brian's colleagues and friends filtered into the pews
behind her. Only one person sat on the other side, to
represent Luisa's family; immediately across the aisle
there was a vague form at the edge of her vision.
Jemma's glazed stare remained rigidly ahead, her brain
numb, blanked out by some merciful process which had
enabled her to handle the events of the last few days.
Yet, despite the fact that she hadn't turned to confirm
her belief, she knew very well who was causing so many
sideways glances aross the aisle, so much shuffling and
whispering. Vasari couldn't go anywhere without
attracting attention.

It was the unexpectedness of his appearance that had
thrown her off balance, she told herself. In a moment,
she'd be as calm inside as she was on the outside. She
would *not* go over the events of the past. It would be
foolish to resurrect her one and only foray into the
treacherous world of love. He was out of her life. This
was an unpleasant but mercifully brief reappearance.
She could weather it.

The colours on the ornate altar cloth swam mistily
before Jemma's eyes as the service proceeded. Through
the thin rendering of 'Abide with Me' she strained her
ears, wondering whether Vasari had the nerve to sing
amid all that isolation.

He hadn't. Not one baritone note. Of course, it might
dent his haughty image if he did anything so human.
Drat! Why couldn't she stop thinking? Remembering so
much of the past made the blood roar in Jemma's head.
Anger swept away her sorrow; wild, unbridled, disturb-
ing anger, that made her beautifully shaped lips tighten

and her blue eyes glint like hard sapphires.

Why had he come? Was he penitent? Did he wish he'd forgiven his cousin Luisa? And if so, why was he here alone, without the rest of the Vasari clan? When her brother Brian had fallen in love with Luisa, Vasari had made it plain that he was against the marriage. The Mortimers weren't good enough for the wealthy and noble Count Vittorio Romano de Vasari di Montevecchio and he had done everything in his power to dissuade Luisa from her course. But true love had won, thought Jemma with a sad smile, and Vasari had driven back to Montevecchio in a filthy temper. From that day, his family had disowned Luisa, refusing any contact. It was typically medieval. The Count revered his twisted sense of honour more than compassion.

The pulse in Jemma's throat suddenly leapt into life, and she had to tighten her defences hastily as she realised why he'd come. She'd almost forgotten: he loved Luisa, of course. Misery clawed at Jemma's mind, and for several minutes she battled to conquer the desire to sink on to the seat and abandon herself to self-pity.

An indescribable force was turning her head. She *mustn't* look. He was too devastatingly handsome, too sensual, and she wanted to keep on hating him, not to find him attractive. But as she told herself this, a perverse drive clamoured to be satisfied, a shamefully spiteful urge to know whether he was actually suffering because of Luisa's death.

Her neck felt stiff, a sure sign that she'd been holding herself more rigidly than she imagined, and she made a conscious effort to drop her shoulders and relax. The desire to look at him, just once, became stronger. Coolly angling her head as though she was examining the choir stalls, she then slanted her eyes in his direction. She trembled, teetering on the elegant high heels, her already quavering voice stopping as if her vocal cords had been cut with a knife.

He'd hardly changed; the impact was just as it had been three years ago: the sheer expensive grooming, the almost regal bearing, the shock of his unusual colouring. The Count's haughty face with its aristocratic nose, scrolling nostrils and sharply defined cheekbones was olive-skinned, as anyone might expect. But in devastating contrast were the brilliant blue eyes and their long fringe of dark lashes. And, even more startling, hair which was the colour of ripe corn. The short, feathery layers capped his head like a yellow mane that was slicked back from his face without even a parting, as if he was aware that the style emphasised the purity of his bone-structure. Vittorio, she thought wryly, knew to a millimetre how to make the most of his admittedly stunning features.

The Vasaris were descended from the fair Plantagenets, who had left a legacy of blond children around the Mediterranean after the Crusades. The Count's ancestor had fought shoulder-to-shoulder with Richard the Lionheart, and had received land in Italy from the grateful King. But it must have been an Italian woman who gave Vittorio his mouth.

Jemma had hardly been able to take her eyes away from its extraordinary sensuality when she first saw him. It was shaped like a cresting wave, curving up extravagantly at each corner even when in repose. The upper lip dipped deeply from the corners, rising to high twin peaks with an appealing dip in the centre. It had made her wonder what it must be like to meet that mouth, lip to lip. Now she wished she'd never known that feeling.

If only she had thought a little more, instead of being totally bewitched by the elegant Count, she would have realised that a man with his lineage wouldn't consider any alliance with the newly rich Mortimers. People like her were fine for a bit of fun, a little light flirtation, but far too unworthy for a serious relationship.

Jemma's eyes narrowed with anger and, at that moment, the Count turned his head and looked at her. He maintained an imperious and aristocratic expression that was typically impossible to read—except for his eyes. In them blazed a hatred so intense, so murderous, that Jemma was transfixed by it, as surely as if he had taken one of his princely ancestor's swords and skewered her heart.

Christobel's hand caught her elbow anxiously. 'Sit down, you look awful,' she whispered hoarsely, her eyes flicking over to the silent menace of the Count's glittering cobalt stare.

Slowly, Jemma tore her gaze away and swallowed to disperse the terrible ache in her throat. The knowledge that he hated her so violently was not only a shock, but somehow made her miserable, too. Loathing him all these years had been her pleasure, her privilege, her right. He had treated her brother and sister-in-law callously. She could understand—but not accept—his fury with Brian, because Luisa had preferred him to the Count, and that must have wounded his Italian pride and caused the spiteful exile.

Jemma frowned. What she couldn't understand was the malevolence that lashed out of his eyes. His contempt was to be expected, however unjustified it was, but it was blatantly unfair to switch his blood feud from Brian to her! It was almost as if he held her responsible for Luisa's death.

Although she told herself that he was small-minded, petty and irrational, none of that seemed to be connecting with her emotions. Deep inside her, she felt devastated to know that the heartless, infuriatingly superior Count looked as if he wanted to take her by the throat and slowly throttle the life out of her.

There was a nudge in her ribs from Christobel.

'Don't worry about me,' muttered Jemma.

Satisfied, Christobel resumed her singing, but not before casting a frankly covetous look at the Count. Jemma lifted her head high, containing the emotions that raged within. No one would know from her cool exterior how unhappy and how angry she felt. Without his presence, she might have given in to her distress and allowed her tears to fall, but as it was she had no intention of showing any signs of weakness. Her grief was private. Vasari was the last man on earth to whom she would expose her raw wounds.

The singing, the words of the vicar, the procession to the grave, all washed over her as if she was living on another planet. It wasn't real, any of this. If she was patient, and kept her head, the nightmare would end. She'd wake to find Brian and Luisa laughing together at the breakfast table, not the victims of a motorway pile-up. Although . . . Jemma's smooth brow was marred by a tiny frown. There hadn't been so much laughter between them lately. The jolly, fun-loving Brian had been unusually subdued. She'd put that down to the fact that he was beginning at last to accept his responsi-bilities, but now an awful premonition entered her mind, adding to her worries. Something was wrong, she knew it.

The pair of black leather Ferragamo shoes swam into view as they advanced to the edge of the grave. Her eyes travelled reluctantly up the long, elegant legs clad in fine black suiting, the jacket flaring subtly over slender hips, the black grosgrain waistcoat and tie swelling out with the powerful chest. There was a flash of yellow as an artistic hand drew something from the jacket pocket, and her eyes followed the small spray of mimosa that landed on Luisa's coffin. The figure turned abruptly and walked away.

'What a nerve that man's got, to show up here,' said Charles sharply, when Jemma had quietly shaken hands with the vicar and the handful of people began to disperse to their cars.

'It's over now,' she said dully. 'I don't have to see him ever again.' She stepped into the waiting limousine.

'You haven't invited him back for tea, then?' asked Christobel, sliding in beside her.

Apart from the Vasaris—and she refused to consider them to be her relatives—Jemma had no family now, and, although Christobel and Charles had only moved next door last year, they had forged a strong bond with the Mortimer family. They were the only people Jemma wanted near her at this time.

She shot a glance at the disappointed Christobel. 'Certainly not,' she said stiffly. 'I'd be betraying Brian if the Count set foot in my house.'

'But he's come all the way from Italy . . .'

'That was his choice,' said Jemma coldly.

'Ye-e-es, but you can't send him back again without even a cup of tea.'

'Yes, I can,' she said calmly, suddenly triumphant at the thought that she could do whatever she liked as far as the Count was concerned. Now *she* could snub *him*.

'He has a right . . .' Christobel blinked a little at the ice in the cornflower eyes behind the black half-veil. Like many people, she was a little in awe of the self-possessed and beautiful Jemma. Her blonde hair was always immaculate and silky, her face pure and untroubled. Tall and perfectly groomed, she seemed unapproachable: too cool, too contained. For the first time, though, that flicker of dislike in Jemma's eyes when she had spoken of the mysterious, glamorous Count and indicated that a lot more went on inside that gorgeous head than people usually imagined.

'He has no right at all! He can't expect to deny that Luisa exists for three years and then come lording it back into my home,' said Jemma in tight, precise tones. 'He made it quite clear that he despises us. I have no intention of being polite to an out-and-out swine.'

She looked straight ahead again, presenting her classic profile. For the hundredth time, Christobel thought how unfair it was that one woman should look so perfect.

'No, but things like weddings and funerals do bring families together again. Perhaps he's prepared to bury the hatchet,' she suggested.

'If that man attempts to approach me,' said Jemma quietly, 'I will bury the hatchet in his arrogant, aristo-cratic skull.'

'Jemma!' remonstrated Charles. 'Think how he must feel! He's probably as upset as you are.'

'Oh, no, not him,' she said in a low voice.

That man didn't have an ounce of real emotion inside

his body. Oh, he displayed a lot, lied with eloquent eyes and that damnable mouth of his, syruping words from his deceitful, flattering lips, but it was all show. He had no depth. Only if he broke his mirror would he be desolate. The Count had but two thoughts in his head: to preserve his family honour at any cost, and to get as many women into his bed as possible.

'The only thing that upsets Vasari, Charles, is any implied slur on his breeding and that high-born family of his. Maybe if he cut himself shaving he'd contemplate suicide for a moment because his beauty had been marred,' she said with icy contempt.

'Jemma, that's not very nice!' Charles sounded astonished.

'Nice? Neither is he. The man was born without a heart. He's like a wooden puppet, except that all his moves are directed by outmoded tradition.'

'Well, I thought he looked pretty cut up when he dropped the flowers on his cousin's coffin,' said Charles.

'So he should,' breathed Jemma, squeezing her fists tightly till the knuckles gleamed white. 'He killed her, after all!'

'Good grief! That's nonsense!' cried Charles. 'You're not yourself, I know, but . . .'

'I am perfectly in control of myself,' she said quietly. 'Vasari was responsible for my brother's death, and Luisa's. If ever I have the opportunity, I'll make him pay for that. He caused us untold misery. One day he'll regret that he snubbed Brian by looking down his noble patrician nose and pronouncing my family unsuitable for marriage into the great house of Vasari!'

Charles stared at her, the slender body held very

upright and untouchable in the black suit that curved in at her waist to continue its sleek lines down the pencil-slim skirt. He kept forgetting that she wasn't that old: under all that confidence was, a twenty-two-year-old who'd lost the brother she hero-worshipped and a gentle sister-in-law she adored. Jemma had always looked more mature than she was because of her poise, and perhaps that had been the trouble. She'd never been able to act her age. He knew from Christobel that Jemma's mother had died when she was very small and that her father treated Jemma like a replacement wife, getting her to act as hostess, the woman of the house, from quite an early age. Desperate to please her unhappy father, she'd put on layers of sophistication too soon, concealing the real girl beneath. And from all accounts, the brief tangle she'd had with the Italian had made her clam up even more. She needed a hug and a cuddle—but Jemma wasn't the sort of girl you cuddled. The reserve, the ice, was too powerful a deterrent.

Jemma was glad that Charles and Christobel left her alone for the rest of the journey home. Almost without realising it, she found herself re-living the events of the summer when she met Vittorio, remembering how annoyed she'd been with Brian when he announced that he'd invited a business contact of their father's to stay.

'A *count!* Oh, really, Brian!' she'd protested, wildly visualising a silvery-haired old man wielding a gold-topped cane and peeling off grey kid gloves to reveal diamond rings on every finger. 'I suppose you'll want me to play hostess. You know how much reading I've got this summer before I start university. I have to do it, you know!'

'To hell with working during the holidays! Have a

bit of fun,' grinned her brother. 'Besides, he's bringing his cousin Luisa along for the Grand Tour of Europe. Wealthy Italians don't consider their education complete till they've girdled the world. He's acting as her protector, so they won't be around all the time if he's taking her sight-seeing.'

'Protector?' That sounded positively Victorian.

'I suppose someone has to make sure that she returns pure and unscathed,' grinned Brian. 'Poor girl, he's probably awfully staid. Father was always extolling his virtues and saying I ought to be more like him. So I'm not mad keen on him coming, either.'

Jemma frowned. Just for once, she'd wanted to be perfectly selfish and prepare herself for her language course. Thinking up ways to amuse a doddery old aristocrat and his cousin wasn't going to be much fun.

'Please, Jems,' Brian coaxed. 'Help me with the old bore. I've tried to run the business since Father died, but I'm making a hash of it. I need to pick the Count's brains and perhaps get him to help clear up the mess.'

Poor Brian. After living the playboy life in Mayfair, he wasn't ready for the discipline that had suddenly been imposed on him. He'd never intended to become involved in their father's Italian property business. In fact, neither of them knew much about it. Father had been a workaholic even before their mother died, and never hid his impatience with her easy-going brother. Brian adored Jemma, who at nineteen was six years his junior, and she loved his happy-go-lucky nature. Their father's sudden death had brought them both up rather sharply, tying them to a common future, although Jemma had always planned to work for her father when she gained her degree in languages. Until then, she could help a little, she supposed.

'OK, I'll do my bit,' she promised, and relief flooded Brian's face. Vasari was more important than she'd thought.

And younger, she discovered: not a doddery old man after all, but an extraordinarily handsome and sexy Italian, escorting a darkly beautiful young girl. In the summer heat, he was wearing an elegant stone-coloured suit in a fine summer-weight linen. It was cut in a very foreign style that looked almost flamboyant and showy, yet was a perfect complement to his manner. His shirt was immaculate, echoing the sharp white of the handkerchief that peeped from his jacket pocket. And his shoes were sand-coloured, to match the suit.

He sat on one of the loungers by the pool, sipping iced lemonade. As he answered Brian's polite enquiries about the journey, Jemma allowed her glance to run idly up the casually stretched legs and over the strong thighs. Jemma had never examined a man in such detail, but then no man had ever remotely met her ideals before. Either they tended to be attractive and immature, or mature and unattractive. She had dozens of boyfriends who flocked to her sophisticated, cool beauty which was unawakened as yet by the stirrings of passion, and was immune to seduction. Jemma was looking for sincerity and commitment, and had no intention of being a notch in someone's bedpost.

She took in the powerful chest and width of shoulder, the golden throat rising above the snowy shirt, and then settled back to watch him as he spoke. Occasionally she responded to a question or a comment addressed to her directly; otherwise she was content just to soak him up. It was like soaking in warm Mediterranean sunshine.

Gradually she became aware that she was comparing Brian to the Count, and finding her brother wanting. Brian's attitude jarred and he sounded too flip, too casual, and unwilling to do more than produce clichés and make smart remarks. Her disloyalty shocked her, but Vittorio had an indefinable quality about him that made all the men she'd known seem very shallow and inadequate. She shifted restlessly, crossing her tanned legs, and found Vittorio's eyes darkening as they watched the movement.

Looking back, she realised that she'd begun to surrender her heart from the moment he bent over her hand and murmured her name in his melodious voice. It was the fact that he seemed interested in her as a person that drew such deep feelings from her wakening heart. He really seemed to care how she felt and what she thought. His courtesy, his consideration and his obvious delight in her company made her sparkle with life. Each evening, before Luisa or Brian came down for dinner, they played piano duets, sitting thigh to thigh on the piano stool, Jemma's hands occasionally faltering in sheer tension till Vittorio lifted them, kissed each finger tenderly and invariably left with a rueful smile.

Conversation at the dinner table became sharper, wittier and more exciting, and Jemma found that she was often passionately defending an idea while Vittorio's clever tongue tried to tie her up in knots. Her insides were in enough knots as it was, when he looked at her with his hooded eyes. As they sparred, joked or listened intently to each other, it seemed that they were heading for a moment when all the silent messages would be impossible to contain any longer and they would both be forced to reveal their feelings.

Through the long, hot summer, she became certain in her own mind that Vittorio was the only man who could fulfil all her dreams, the lifetime lover she had been waiting for, the reason she had never succumbed to the entreaties of the young men who breathed hot promises into her ear.

Life was building up to a crescendo, and for Jemma that moment was near. She'd seen how he kissed the hands of other women and flattered them; how affectionate he was to Luisa. Was it only to her that his drowsy eyes spoke of love and desire? She had to be sure, and there was only one way to find out: push him too far, because she couldn't bear the suspense any longer.

At the end of the summer he would be returning to Italy. As the days flew by at an alarming rate, Jemma made plans. She knew he found her alluring; his whole manner told her so, and she was sure that only his innate sense of honour as a guest in their house was putting a brake on their relationship.

After dinner one evening, she had wandered into the music room, leaving the others drinking coffee. She had given Vittorio a long look as she left, hoping he'd follow. Nervously, she sat down at the piano and fingered the keys, waiting.

'Jem-ma,' murmured Vittorio's expensive brandy voice. 'You look very beautiful this evening. Your eyes and your dress are the same blue as the stained-glass window in our family church. I've always thought it to be an astonishing colour. Perhaps I should carry you there, to make sure my memory isn't playing me false.'

He was lounging in the doorway, dressed casually in a pair of fine dove-grey Milanese linen trousers and an open-necked white shirt. His jacket hung around his shoulders like a cape, and Jemma felt her heart begin to hammer unevenly. The skin at his throat was darkly golden, the sleeves rolled up to powerful biceps displaying strongly corded arms and a wrist encircled by a heavy gold watch.

This was the moment, she knew it. 'I'd like that. I've always wanted to be abducted by a man of impulse,' she said, letting her eyes flirt.

He smiled. 'You would leave your home for a man you hardly know?'

She had the impression that he was casting around for encouragement. 'Some people you feel you've known all your life,' she said quietly.

'So it is with us,' he murmured, his voice husky. 'But I would still like to know you better.'

Jemma felt the tension between them mounting. If only he wasn't so polite! 'Then why don't you go ahead?' she asked with a nervous tremor to her lips.

Vittorio straightened, suddenly very still, and it seemed they looked at one another for an eternity.

'Careful,' he said, his voice husky. 'Don't give me any opportunities to take our relationship further unless you really know what you're letting yourself in for. I'm finding it hard enough to restrain myself as it is. I can remain a polite guest providing I'm not encouraged to break rules.'

'Rules?' she breathed, dismissing them. 'Are you so tied by convention?'

'Not at all.' His eyes become almost navy in their dark intensity, glittering with an inner light. 'The rules help control passionate men like me. But there are certain things that made me break rules. *Gesù!*' he breathed, as she stared at him, wide-eyed. 'I think I had better leave.'

'No! Please . . .' She rose, the silk of her full-skirted dress rustling softly. Vittorio's eyes rested on her slender waist, lingered meltingly on her gently rising breasts, and Jemma found her skin tingling on her naked shoulders as if his hands, not his eyes, were touching them. 'Are you bored with me?'

He frowned. 'You know perfectly well that's not the reason I'm leaving.'

Jemma's face lit with an inner joy. 'Leaving? Then why are you still standing there?' she gurgled. Vittorio's mouth twisted in a wry smile and she arched an eyebrow at him. But his face had become watchful and there was a lurking sensuality in his expression that wiped away her amused confidence and replaced it with a warm lassitude.

'You are a tease! Don't look at me like that!' he growled, advancing a little.

'Like what?' she whispered, knowing how her whole expression was telling him that she wanted his kiss.

With a barely stifled groan, he began to walk towards her, holding her eyes with his own, a look of raw emotion within them. He paused, a short distance away, his chest rising and falling in time with the soft sound of his breath that came from his parted lips.

'Jemma . . .' His eyes clouded with desire as they toured her body, and her hand rose with an involuntary movement to her breast to stem the fierceness of the knives that shafted there. 'Should I return to Brian and Luisa?' he asked quietly.

He was permitting her to control the situation. Jemma trembled at the demand in the look he gave her. 'No.'

His lashes swept his cheeks and then rose again. As he neared, it seemed natural that Jemma should lift her arms and be drawn against his strong chest. His heart was thudding as wildly as hers. In his embrace, she felt as if she had come home. This was the moment and the man she'd always been waiting for, and now she had found him her life could really begin. He was lifting her chin to gaze into her eyes, and she allowed her feelings to be read clearly.

'I've been longing to kiss you for days,' he breathed. The blue eyes were as deep as the Pacific, and she began to drown.

His hand stole around the back of her neck, to that warm, sensitive area beneath the hair that flowed over his fingers like wild, white silk. The slow and insidious rhythm as he massaged her nape sent her heart lurching unevenly, and a wonderful lassitude was closing her eyes and parting her lips. Then his carved mouth descended, repeating her name over and over again with that slow, heart-stopping murmur. Their lips met, softly warm, and his arms tightened, enfolding her with a quick movement so that their bodies melded into one. Heat ran between them in a melting line, fusing them together, searing their nerve-endings and sending them both a little crazy as Vittorio's mouth moved passionately over hers. It was like touching a chord for the first time, and discovering harmony.

Jemma relaxed, abandoning herself willingly to his increasingly insistent caresses, wanting him to know that she, too, was passionate and could match his desire. He responded with a savagery that at first alarmed her, till she caught his urgency and returned his kisses eagerly. She welcomed his fire, and was not afraid when he drew her down on to the soft peach carpet. With a low, impatient growl, he pushed her back and stretched his powerful body across her, shifting his thighs deliberately to tell her of his arousal. She wasn't shocked. She was falling in love.

'Kiss me again,' she breathed.

'I should stop,' he said. 'But I need to touch you.' His breath rasped in his throat as Jemma's fingers traced his crested mouth in wonder, his hooded eyes glinting under the thick lashes. She slid her finger across the hollow of his cheek and investigated the smooth, silken skin behind his ear.

Vittorio's reaction startled her. With a low moan, he hauled her body hard against his, then pressed his whole weight downwards till her spine felt every crushed fibre of the shaggy carpet. Sensations rocketed through her: the fierce, relentless grinding of his mouth, his harsh breathing, the hard strength of his body and the heat it was generating. Every part of her was exulting that they had cast away the barriers and could begin the magical exploration between one man and one woman. Her arms stole around his neck and she dug her fingers into his glorious golden hair, letting its silk add another sensory experience to all the others. The thrust of his loins became more insistent, and desire speared her body.

'God! I want you!' he muttered thickly.

'Oh, Vittorio,' she breathed in triumph, clutching his shoulders.

Then came the sound of Brian's laughter on the stairs in the hall. With a stifled oath, Vittorio rolled over, leant across to drop a tender kiss on her lips and sat up reluctantly, his breathing ragged, his eyes dark with hunger.

'That will teach me not to wait till we have guaranteed privacy,' he rasped, his long fingers caressing her tumbling hair. He held out a hand to help her up.

Jemma felt herself grow cold. He'd made it sound as though the whole episode had been purely physical. She raised troubled eyes to him, but he was intent on fastening the buttons of his shirt. With shaking hands she began to smooth her dress, and found his brooding eyes following her hands.

'May God help me!' he cried, pulling her towards him. 'I can't leave you alone!' He took her mouth in one last bruising kiss, before pushing her away harshly. 'Tonight, Jemma,' he said, the raw ache in his voice making her body light up again. 'Let me come to you. Don't ask me to hold back, because I can't. And I'm not giving you a chance to think, in case you run out on me. You know what there is between us; it's been building up over the weeks, despite my efforts to remain detached. You should never have encouraged me,' he smiled. 'Now it's too late, the inevitable has happened. I knew from the first moment I set eyes on you that it would come to this. I warn you that I am not one of those haunted young men who hang around the house, willing to be enslaved while you sacrifice only a brief hour. I don't follow rules when I'm aroused. I take what I need and I'm greedy. I want everything you have to give. Do you understand what I'm saying, *amore? Everything!*'

It was a threat, a promise, a warning . . . Jemma didn't know what to think. Brian's steps were in the hall and Vittorio hurried to the door. Her eyes were huge as she watched him leave, blowing her a kiss from his fingers.

'Till tonight,' he murmured, turning, his words low and caressing. At that moment, Brian called him. He sighed, shrugged eloquently and strode away, leaving Jemma in a ferment of doubt.

Suddenly, in the space of a few minutes, everything had become confused and she was uncertain of his motives. It was as if she'd leapt on a galloping horse and expected it to walk sedately with her, until she was ready to progress. Vittorio obviously wasn't used to reins, once he'd been given his head. Now he expected to make love to her. His interest was purely physical. A repressed Italian, unable to slake his lust with the carefully guarded women of his race, he was behaving abroad like an amorous athlete. She'd honestly expected kisses, a little loving, to be held tenderly and talked to, and then a reluctant and sweet leavetaking. Then gradually, as the days went by, they'd learn more about each other, physically, emotionally, mentally, till they were both ready to make some kind of declaration. That was how it happened. Those were the ground rules.

Well, she told herself, he'd already told her that he flouted rules. Like a fool, she'd misinterpreted his messages. Jemma sighed. Tonight she would lock her door. There was something sordid and humiliating about losing your virginity to a man you were infatuated with, but who wanted only your body.

Half the night she lay propped up in bed, watching the door-handle. It never turned; there was no soft knock, no pleading. In the morning, she discovered why.

'*Gone?*' she repeated in shock.

'Yes. I've blown it,' said Brian. 'I told Vasari that

Luisa and I love each other.'

Jemma was amazed. Too involved in her relationship with Vittorio, she hadn't realised the implications behind the way they had always paired off.

'You should have seen the way he reacted,' continued Brian gloomily. 'Like a jealous lover. White with rage, he was! Hissed a lot, clenched his fists a lot, and stormed off to take Luisa away to talk sense into her. They've gone to the Lake District, I think. He left a message for you.'

'W-w-what was it?' she asked, nausea clawing at her stomach.

'Oh, I dunno,' said Brian vaguely. 'Sent his regards or something, apologised and said he'd be back. My God, Jems, if he marries Luisa, I'll kill him!'

'Marries . . .!'

'I told you, he was stamping mad. I obviously pinched his girl. It figures. That sort always marry their own kind. Luisa's probably been groomed to be his bride ever since childhood without realising it.'

'Oh, Brian!' she breathed, dropping down into a chair. 'I thought . . . I admired him, I—I thought I loved him.'

He snorted. 'You and the rest of the world. I'm sorry,' he said hastily, as he saw her eyes filling with unshed tears. 'I'm hurting so much inside. You must be, too. Jems, I can't bear you to cry. Stop it, for heaven's sake! Listen,' he said, when she continued to sob, 'forget him. He's not worth your tears.' He stared at her in exasperation, hating to see his sister upset. 'Vasari is an out-and-out rake, after any woman who gives him the glad eye, and plenty do.'

Jemma lifted her head and looked at him doubtfully.

'He's not like that——'

'Jems, this may come as a shock to you, but many men are like that.'

'No . . .'

'Yes.' She was still shaking her head, as if that would give the lie to his words. 'Come on, poppet, you can't love a man who goes tom-catting around the moment he's away from his family!'

She froze. Love left her heart faster than it had entered. She gave a silent cry. The greedy Count wanted everything all right. Everything women had to give him. Well, he wasn't having *her*.

For days the atmosphere in the house was depressing. To her intense irritation, Brian threw a wild party to cheer himself up, and Jemma was miserably trying to get some sleep despite the people blundering about the house playing 'Murder in the Dark'. Her bedroom door was locked, but the one connecting her bathroom to Brian's was not, and consequently Brian's Rugby Club friend barged in, flinging himself on the bed in delight to find her there.

'Out! Dave, what . . .'

'Shut up, Jems,' Dave breathed. 'They'll find us.'

Appalled that all she wore was a flimsy, low-cut nightdress, she struggled to escape the large hand over her mouth. From downstairs came the sound of men arguing, their voices carrying above the loudspeaker that was blaring out pop music. Dave's body had trapped her, allowing his free hand to roam over her breasts. Jemma began to panic, moaning and panting beneath his sweaty palm.

Suddenly, the light snapped on and she saw Vittorio, standing in an attitude of shock in the bathroom doorway. She realised with a sick feeling that her breathing was heavy, her breasts partially spilling from the lacy bodice.

'Put the light out, chum,' complained Dave. 'Can't you see we're in the middle of . . .'

'Yes,' came Vittorio's hiss.

She lay in frozen horror, paralysed by the sheer violence of his expression. The proud head was held high in the bright glare, the hard light casting harsh shadows under his eyes and in the hollow of his cheekbones. His nostrils quivered with barely controllable breathing, and his beautiful mouth had been robbed of its sensual lines by the contempt that shaped his words.

'I'm sorry, Jemma. Forgive me for intruding. I'm unused to couples who have sex with one of the doors open. I should have remembered that you and your brother don't have the morals of the Vasari house. Excuse me. My cousin seems to want your kind of life and nothing I say can persuade her otherwise. But I'll leave this den of vice, before I am corrupted against my will and I, too, descend into hell!'

CHAPTER TWO

THE cortège drove through the exclusive stockbroker belt as Jemma re-lived the way she had rounded on the astonished Dave. So icy, so biting were her words that her tone, vibrating with disgust and emotion, had chilled his passion and crushed his ego. All her misery and lost hopes were flung into reviling him. In the face of her stony expression and withering scorn, he had made a hasty exit. That incident laid the foundations for her cool reputation, since Dave made sure his inaccurate version was related to his male friends.

Some of those men were here—but not Dave, thought Jemma in relief, as she greeted people in the entrance hall. Mrs Parks, the housekeeper, kept an eye on the unobtrusive waitresses with their trays of sherry and dainty snacks, and Jemma was thankfully relieved of every duty other than accepting the murmurs of sympathy. Most of these people she hardly knew. From the way some of them were dressed, Brian had a number of bookie friends. Polite, restrained, she shook hands with everyone and kept her thoughts to herself.

In fact, her mind was dulled. She hadn't even thought what to do with the business—whether to take it over, or find someone to replace Brian . . . She nodded vaguely at a stocky man in a camelhair overcoat, who asked if he could have a word with her soon. There was an accountant hovering around somewhere, who'd been trying to speak to her for the last two days. She'd have to face him, too, and eventually take up the reins, but for the moment he'd have to wait. One step at a time.

At last there seemed to be no more visitors arriving, and Jemma was about to join her guests when the gravel crunched harshly under screaming tyres. Frowning slightly, her mouth tightening in irritation at the new arrival's bad manners, she moved to the open door. Her eyes widened in shock. Damn Vasari!

His long legs slid from the low-slung Ferrari and crossed the drive. Jemma's eyes filled with scorn. His car was certainly an extension of his personality: sleek, racy, elegant and polished, with a fast acceleration that left you breathless, and an incomparable holding power on curves. Both were equally dangerous, equally tuned to perfection, equally able to rev up and disappear into the mid-distance, leaving trembling bodies in their wake.

It dawned on her that he must have driven through the night from his *palazzo* in Montevecchio to reach them in time for the funeral. Her lip curled. Stubborn as ever! He'd once said that flying was an uncivilised way to travel. Because of his pig-headed, antique beliefs, he had knocked himself out by driving a thousand miles unnecessarily. Typical. And he'd be driving straight back again, if she had anything to do with it. Avoiding direct eye-contact, Jemma assumed a regal expression. Cool, calm control was something she had perfected over the years. No longer could she be bowled over by his effortless charm. She realised that unconsciously she'd been preparing for this moment. There would be no crack in her façade for him to see, nothing that would give him the opportunity to feel superior.

'*Il Conte de Vasari,* you are not welcome in this house,' she said coldly, her head high on her long, swanlike neck, her remote eyes fixed on the knot of his black tie.

There was a pause, during which she knew from her peripheral vision that his jaw was clenching.

'Good afternoon, Jemma,' came his perfectly modulated voice as he held out his hand in greeting.

Immediately she was thrown back into the past. The years disappeared as if they had never been. The resonant tones had deepened a little, but were still mellow-brown, and the way he said her name, separating the double 'm' in a murmur that bordered on a hum, was music to her love-starved ears. And were his words drifting from that sensual mouth that she had once likened to the crest of a wave? A small tremor disturbed her composure, and she sought refuge in hardness, ignoring the hand, rejecting his false courtesy, reminding herself that this was the man who had killed her brother.

'Get off my land.' Amazing how calm she sounded, how unemotional, when inside she was a churning, seething stew! He had winced at her directness, she was pleased to see. *Il Conte* disliked hard, abrupt speech. His own usually flowed like a melody.

'Your land?' He gave a derisive laugh. 'I regret having to say this so baldly, Jemma, since I was hoping to break the news gently, but you leave me no choice. You see, the unfortunate truth is that it is not for you to send me away. It's a pity you have not spoken with your accountant. This I discovered when I telephoned him from Paris this morning. *Allora,* I have to tell you that this is *my* land. I own it, and the house, and everything in it. Everything. So, let's go inside and act like civilised human beings, shall we?'

His house? Impossible! Slowly her head lifted, a fraction of an inch at a time, till at last she looked straight at him and momentarily forgot the bombshell of his words. For long seconds she swam in his blue ocean depths, and she was reminded of her infatuation and the night he had kissed her.

Her vision blurred and a black wall seemed to come straight up from the floor to engulf her. Strong arms caught her up, and she registered dizzily that the Count had lifted her, with one muscled arm under her slim knees, the other curving intimately around her back. She fought for consciousness in order that she might escape his arrogant takeover, weak, furious and shaking with impotence as he strode into the hallway and a buzz of chatter. Her limbs were heavy, her head whirled as if she was drunk and she could support it no longer, so that it fell right back, exposing her vulnerable throat.

Shock had finally hit her. A treacherous longing to abandon all her responsibilities and let Vasari handle the next few hours swept over her. Then she was immediately ashamed of such feebleness and stirred in his arms, trying, as she did so, not to clutch at his broad chest for support. Of anyone here, it would have to be Vasari who'd swept her into his arms! Giddily, she caught his lapels and tried to pull herself up, but the blackness descended again and she sank limply back.

'Move aside,' he ordered in clear, ringing tones, stamping his authority on everyone within earshot. '*Signorina,* you work for Miss Mortimer? Bring some brandy.'

His long legs devoured two steps at a time, and

Jemma's fuddled brain registered that he was heading for her bedroom.

'No!' she managed, her eyes frightened, yet avoiding his in the knowledge that they'd frighten her more. She reached in panic for the mahogany banister in an attempt to halt their progress. He drew her away with a swift movement.

'But yes,' he grated through clenched teeth. 'You can recover and I will explain the situation. It will be an excellent opportunity to talk to you, Jemma,' he said. His voice became harsher. 'Now, if I remember, your room is to the right? The carpet is badly worn from all those feet that have hurried to your door.'

'You——!' Jemma wriggled ineffectually, but stopped at his mocking laugh as she realised that he was finding her movement in his arms enjoyable.

'Please continue to fight me, Jemma,' he murmured. 'I rather enjoy watching you arch your lovely body.'

'Put me down!' she said shakily, feeling far too weak to stand if he obeyed. She had no wish to remember the last time he had been in her bedroom. Instead, she tried to remember what had he said just now. Something about the house? She felt so helpless with her brain spinning in crazy circles.

'I'd be delighted to put you down, but then I would have to drag you along the floor, since you are too weak to walk, and I am too much of a gentleman to treat you so badly. Please don't imagine that I find pleasure in holding you,' he said contemptuously. 'Rest assured that I would never insult my good taste by making advances to you. If you risked a glance at my face, you'd find dislike there.' He waited, but she kept her lashes low to conceal the misery that coursed unexpectedly through her brain. With a brief, mirthless laugh, he pushed open her bedroom door.

Four strides took him to her bed. As if relinquishing a soiled bundle of washing, he lowered his arms and rolled her on to the black satin counterpane. The house had been lavishly decorated and furnished during the last two years, and Jemma had given in to Brian's outrageous ideas of glamour.

Having a bedroom in black and gold had seemed fun at the time. Now, she felt the Count's scornful gaze roving with insolent appraisal over her body and also its setting, that suddenly seemed rather tackily opulent now he was here.

Jemma squashed the inferior feeling. Angry at being treated so dispassionately, she was also disconcerted to find that her dignity had been ruffled. For her black toque was askew and her skirt had rucked up over her knees. She tore off the hat and flung it away. In doing so, her hair unravelled and tumbled in thick white-blonde waves on to her shoulders.

Vasari hissed in his breath and his eyes narrowed. Unnerved, and exhausted by emotion, Jemma lay back on the pillows, her whole body trembling.

'Hmm. Very glamorous, very tragic,' he sneered. 'The cool queen of beauty, totally aware of the fact that she looks her best against black. It is such a pity, Jemma, that you do not have a mirror to see what I am enjoying. Ah, here is one.'

He was angling her huge hand mirror above her. Reflected, she cold see the soft glint of her released tresses spreading wantonly over the glossy black satin. It seemed that her eyes stood out in her pale face, glowing a deep sky-blue, huge and startled, fringed by her carefully mascaraed navy lashes. Vasari tilted the mirror and there was her body, neat, svelte, the tiny wasp waist emphasising the curve of her hips. Then, with a shock, she saw the immodest, long, long length of smooth, slim legs, revealed by her rumpled skirt.

'There, don't you find the sight of yourself pleasing?' he mocked.

'God! I hate you!' she said fervently. She sat up and dragged the skirt into place with a closed expression. 'I hate you so much you make me feel physically sick!'

'Indeed.' His eyes impaled her with their expression of pure menace. 'Then we are in competition. For I feel the same way about you.'

He flicked back his jacket and pushed his hands into his pockets, and Jemma tried not to let her eyes drift to the spread of his chest and his lean, muscled waist. Or his narrow hips. It was an arrogant pose, and it roused in her a stomach-churning anger—and a hot wave of desire at the sexuality of his virile body.

He smiled, a slow, icy smile, as though he knew of the struggle within her. 'It was ill-mannered of you, Jemma,' he said softly, 'to telex a message through to my Florence office saying that Luisa had been killed in an accident. And then to refuse to accept my calls.'

She shot a nervous look at his implacable face. Anger had hardened his mouth and she shivered at the threat he presented. 'I didn't want to speak to you,' she said coldly. 'You hurt the people I loved.'

There was a frigid silence.

'I've brought the brandy, sir.' One of the hired maids hovered in the doorway, all eyes—for Vasari, of course.

Jemma gave an impatient sigh. Looks, looks, looks! her brain screamed. That was all he had! That was all he'd ever had!

He took the tray from her. 'Please leave the door open,' he said sharply, as the maid left.

'Well,' remarked Jemma icily, accepting the brandy. 'Refusing an opportunity for seduction? You *have* changed. Once it was anything in a skirt. Lost your libido with age, have you?'

The Count's expression rose several notches on the Distaste Scale. Jemma shut her eyes in an effort to concentrate on fighting the hollow, empty feeling that his scorn had created.

'I have my desires,' he said tightly. 'I detest the idea of being alone with you. I am wary of voracious, promiscuous women.'

Jemma bridled. He'd seen her in a compromising situation and had never given her the chance to explain. On that one piece of evidence he'd judged her—he, who had seduced half the women in London, according to Brian!

'Get out!' she snapped.

'Not yet. When I have said what I need to say.'

Coldly ignoring him, she opened her lids a fraction and tossed back the drink, desperate to escape from him, desperate not to be humiliated ever again. The alcohol made her feel as if her bones were fashioned from cotton wool, and she lay back with a small gasp.

'How weak you are! When did you last eat? You are as slender as a reed.'

Jemma puzzled. It had been some time ago. 'I don't remember,' she said shakily. No wonder she hardly had the strength to combat his nerve-racking presence. 'Go away,' she muttered.

'In a moment, but first tell me what to have sent up to

you. Someone can bring you a tray. You must eat.'

'No. All I want is to see the back of you,' she said wearily. 'I don't want anything.'

'Ah, the starvation diet,' he said cynically. 'It would not do, to spoil your model-girl figure, would it?' he asked with heavy irony.

The bed depressed and she froze with fear, willing her face not to betray her. A finger reached up and touched her cheekbone lightly, drawing backwards and forwards in sinister threat. In fact, it was so threatening, that a strange feeling ran through her body, trickling the fear hotly to the pit of her stomach and making her pulse beat rapidly.

'How easy it would be,' he continued silkily, his cool breath fanning her face, 'to damage this beautiful skin. A sudden accident, and . . .'

In terrified, jerky movements, her head turned towards him as she tried to read his expression. There was an odd light in his eyes. How serious was he? This haughty, ruthless Italian was autocratic enough to believe that he was some kind of demi-god, able to mete out rewards and punishments like a medieval feudal lord. She knew that despite the veneer of utter politeness he possessed a vicious hunger for revenge that was strong enough to contemplate disfiguring her for life.

Panic-stricken, she tried to speak. Her lips parted obediently, but no sound came from them. She was conscious of anxiety filling her big blue eyes and Vasari's eyes glowing in response. With an angry snarl, he rose abruptly and stared down at her, his face tight with barely leashed fury.

'I will talk to you when you have recovered,' he said, his proud mouth thin and hard. 'Not when you lie there like a seductress and therefore have the advantage over me. Even on the day you bury your brother, you can't prevent yourself from flaunting your sexuality! Tempt someone else, Jemma! I prefer women with principles!'

With a stiff, courtly bow that mocked her with its respect, he swung on his heel and strode from the room, closing the door softly behind him.

Jemma's body slumped. What an arrogant swine he was! He seemed to think that every woman was after him, that every breath she took was calculated to entice him. How *dared* he accuse her like that? She checked her mounting anger. However much his behaviour irritated her, she owed it to her own pride to remain cool and collected, even if she wanted to scream at him and break down his air of supreme disdain, to shatter that irritating certainty that ignored all opposition to his views.

Sexuality! Jemma's mouth tightened. Since getting her fingers burnt by the worldly Count, she'd been totally turned off the idea of sex. That hadn't made her very popular at university. Even casual friendships with men she'd regarded with caution, not wanting to risk becoming too attached to any of them, as she had with Vasari. Corny as it was, her nickname, 'The Ice Queen', was well earned. Until her wounds had healed, she intended to keep her image. It protected her. With any luck, she'd never again be hurt by the whiplash of a man's contempt.

Vasari had spoiled what should have been the best time of her life, and finally destroyed Brian and Luisa. Jemma's teeth bit deep into her lower lip, the stirrings of revenge beginning to sour her mind. She hated him enough to do anything.

'Are you there, dear? Can I come in?'

Jemma stared at the tray of tea and sandwiches which Mrs Parks was placing by the bed.

'That interfering man! I told him I didn't want anything to eat,' she complained.

'He seemed concerned, Jemma,' said Mrs Parks anxiously. 'What lovely manners he has! Fair takes your breath away, doesn't he?'

'You can say that again,' muttered Jemma. 'But don't be fooled. His manners disguise a crawling snake.'

'Oh, my dear! That doesn't sound like you at all! The Count seems . . .'

'Vasari isn't what he seems,' said Jemma. 'That's what I keep telling people, but they never believe me; he lies with such soft conviction.'

'But . . .'

'Please,' Jemma begged. 'I don't want to think about any of it now. Let me get through the ordeal of speaking to everyone downstairs.'

'His nibs said you'd be staying up here . . .'

'His nibs,' said Jemma grimly, 'is far too big for his boots. I feel well enough to face up to my duties.' She rose from the bed with Mrs Parks hovering nervously while she tidied her hair and straightened her clothes.

For a moment, nobody noticed her reappearance. Vasari was holding court, enthralling a large group of people which included, Jemma saw to her dismay, Charles and Christobel. They, too, had been bowled over by his good looks and silver tongue.

All the while she moved around the room, talking to friends and avoiding Vasari skilfully, she was uncomfortably aware of the fact that his eyes frequently strayed in her direction. It was an odd feeling, knowing someone was observing her so intently. Soon it began to make her nervous, and people had to repeat their remarks, because she was finding it difficult to concentrate. She would hear a soft phrase, a deep murmur, maybe, and found to her annoyance that she was actually straining to identify his voice. Her head began to pound unbearably, all her nerve-endings stretched to screaming point. If she didn't relieve the throbbing in her temples, she'd disgrace herself by doing something awful. For a wild moment, she saw herself running over to him, pure hatred disfiguring her face, as she launched herself at him and tore her nails down his smooth, golden cheekbones.

Her eyes closed and she swayed. 'Would you excuse me?' she murmured to Brian's tearful secretary who had been talking to her. As she forced herself to walk normally towards the kitchen, it seemed that she had been on her feet for days. Her calf muscles and the small of her back ached terribly.

Her face was beginning to ache, too, with the effort of maintaining a remote, polite smile, accepting words of sympathy from numerous strange women and listening to Brian's male friends who'd become bored with being quietly polite and were discussing cars they'd bought, shows they'd seen and acts they'd caught at the latest nightspots. She hadn't realised just how much he'd been gadding about on the days he'd spent in London each week. A cold feeling crept in to chill her blood. Vasari couldn't be right, could he, about owning her house?

Impatiently, she shook off the idea. Not by one word had Brian indicated that all was not well.

She half filled a glass and dropped in two aspirins,

mesmerised by the fizzing. Somehow she must get up enough strength to stand up to Vasari and throw him out. Jemma swilled the water around, as the tablets gradually dissolved. Today was turning into a nightmare. She was going to miss Brian and his happy-go-lucky nature. He was always such fun. His secretary had just been telling her, in a broken little voice, how she missed him and her life wasn't the same.

In the act of lifting the glass to her lips, Jemma paused, playing back that conversation and recalling the desperate light in the girl's eyes. Had Brian's secretary been unusually disturbed by his death? Could he . . .? Jemma swallowed the drink, angry with herself for doubting her brother. The girl missed him because he was jolly and friendly and made jokes. She missed his hearty laughter and affectionate way of larking around. Maybe the girl had imagined herself a little bit in love with her boss, but Brian loved Luisa, despite being away so much—that was apparent from the frequent presents he gave her, and the many parties they gave.

'Miss Mortimer?'

Jemma swung around guiltily, as though her thoughts had been discovered. Her face became a polite mask. It was one of the bookies. 'I think we'd better have that little talk now.' The stocky man had placed his hand on her shoulder in a very proprietorial way, as though he was preventing her from escaping from his clutches.

'Impossible now,' she said with some distaste, moving from under his restraining hand. 'You can see I need to circulate. I must rejoin my guests.'

'Me and my colleagues have got one or two things we need settling before the end of the day,' he said, stepping in front of her. The scent of his aftershave made her feel sick. And she'd detected a threat in the man's voice.

'No, I can't, I——' Her voice showed the panic she felt. There was something menacing about his manner, and she looked up with relief when someone else came into the room—only to turn away in irritation when she discovered it was the Count.

'Jemma.' Vasari's arm slid around her shoulders in a protective warmth. She tried to move away but his deceptively relaxed fingers bit deep and she stopped short in surprise. What were these two men after? 'You're looking pale again,' he continued. 'Do you not think a little fresh air might be of benefit?'

'I was talking to the lady first,' protested the bookie.

The Count paused, a little theatrically, and looked him up and down very slowly, projecting the maximum of insult. 'And of course, I am sure, since you appear to be a sensitive, perceptive man, you will have noticed that Miss Mortimer is finding this a difficult experience.' He smiled charmingly. 'I will take her for a stroll in the garden and then you can be sure of her full attention when she returns. With your permission?'

What was it about the Count, thought Jemma, that made him sound so polite—almost deferential—and yet utterly, utterly, ruthless? Perhaps it was the decisive way he dropped his voice at the end of every sentence, even with some questions. It made him sound extraordinarily masculine and sure of himself.

Jemma almost giggled at the bookie's face. He'd been thwarted, but he obviously didn't see how. Torn between relief at being free of the man, bewilderment that she should feel secure with Vasari, and anger at his cool mastery of the situation, Jemma temporarily allowed herself to be led outside, on to the patio. Vasari's hand had slipped to the small of her back, and he was propelling her down the steps, along the path and towards the summer-house, which basked in the gentle spring sunshine.

She stopped dead in the middle of the path, refusing to be pushed along any further. She'd got rid of one unpleasant type; now it was time to cold-shoulder the other.

'Thank you for rescuing me,' she said, her face frozen into an attitude of dislike. 'And now, if you don't mind, I prefer to seek the company of friends.'

With a swift movement, he barred her way. '*After* we have spoken together.'

'Count . . .'

'Vittorio. You always called me that, Jemma,' he said in his musical voice.

'That was before we became enemies,' she said coolly, turning her profile to him in a gesture of indifference.

He gave a mocking laugh. 'So it was. Nevertheless, if I am to tell you about that bookmaker, it would make it easier if we were not on such formal terms.'

'Bookmaker?' She'd been right! What had Brian done?

'Vittorio.'

She shrugged. 'Oh, very well. It's unimportant to me what I call you——' she paused, as though weighing her words carefully '—to your *face*.' The Count's upper lip quivered fractionally. 'What's all this about a book-maker?' she asked casually.

'You need to sit down first,' he said infuriatingly.

'No, I don't! Tell me what you know and then I can leave you. I find my skin crawling even when you're at a distance of ten paces, let alone this close.'

'As you wish,' he said with a sigh. 'But I don't like to make such a sudden revelation without preparing you. But then you always were impatient, Jemma. You wanted something, you had it.'

His cynical eyes held hers as he taunted her, a haughty lift of his eyebrow emphasising his contempt. Jemma flushed to recall how eager she must have seemed when he kissed her, and shrugged her shoulders casually to dispel the sudden sharp longing that permeated her body.

'I almost envy you and your brother your lack of conscience,' he murmured.

'At least we were always loyal to each other,' she rapped.

Vittorio froze, his eyes becoming opaque. Then his lashes fluttered on his cheeks and lifted to reveal that hard, malevolent hatred again.

'You were a fool to be loyal,' he said in a hoarse whisper. 'Blind belief in someone can be dangerous. Now you have to cope with the men who have come to collect Brian's gambling debts. Today. They're not the sort of men who will respect your grief, Jemma. In fact, they are trading on that, knowing that you are at your weakest. If a woman without emotion *can* be weak, that is.'

Her chin tilted stubbornly, a hollow feeling scouring the pit of her stomach. She wouldn't give him the satisfaction of knowing that his words had horrified her. Brian did go to the races frequently, but always seemed cheerful when he came home, and she'd assumed that

he'd had a small flutter and been lucky. Debt was
something that had never figured in her family's
vocabulary; it was shaming. She tried to tell herself that
they were small debts, and that the bookies were merely
being money-wise in collecting them before Brian's
money officially became hers and there was the danger
that she might decide to blue it all on something
frivolous. They were protecting their interests,
naturally. A deep vein of common sense and a flash of
intuition told her that this was not the case, and that a
large sum was involved. Those men looked too angry
and determined to be bothering about a hundred
pounds or so. She swallowed nervously.

'Are you claiming debts, too? Does the business owe
you a couple of pounds?' she asked scathingly.

He swung her around, gripping her arms and forcing
her to look into his eyes. She recoiled from the
animosity that blazed there. The remarkably controlled
Count was rattled.

'The debt that I am owed cannot be paid,' he said
with soft menace, giving her a little shake. 'It's far too
great. You and your family owe me so much . . .' He
paused, lowering his thick lashes over hooded eyes. 'A
little of the debt will be paid soon, I guarantee that.'

'I don't understand,' she said sharply, suddenly wary.
'Explain yourself.'

'How sad that this beautiful body encloses such a
cold, heartless woman,' he muttered, ignoring her
request. Instead he seemed momentarily hypnotised by
her, his thumbs idly rotating over the smooth skin of her
arms. Astonished, she pushed against his chest and he
immediately released her, the cynical look in his eyes
replacing what she had thought was very nearly one of

desire. But then, Vasari had always been a womaniser.

'If you think you're going to comfort me in *that* way,' she said scornfully, 'then forget it. Say what you have to say about Brian, and stop wrapping up your words in fancy parcels.'

'It depresses me, the way you English use words only as a means to communicate facts and information,' said Vittorio. 'They can convey so much more. Still, if you like . . . This is what you must do. I want you to leave those men to me. Tell them that I will settle the matter.'

'You'll what? I'll do no such thing!' she cried. 'I can make all the necessary arrangements to pay any of Brian's debts. I don't need you.'

'I'm afraid you do,' he said with maddening calm. 'There is no money in your account, and certainly none in your brother's.'

'How dare you cast such a slur on my family's financial stability?' she snapped. 'You can't possibly know about our affairs!' So that was the name of the game! He was going around spreading gossip so that the Mortimer name was dragged in the mud! The lying hound! He obviously wanted to hurt her very badly.

'But I do,' he said firmly. 'This has obviously come as a great surprise. I wouldn't have burdened you if it could have been avoided, Jemma, but the fact remains that the men are here and you have to know something of the problems you face. Now, your father opened an account for you, so that you could draw money to see you through university, did he not?'

'I—anyone could work that one out,' she said, battling to remain calm. 'I didn't have any money of my own, and it's perfectly obvious that I wouldn't be eligible for a grant.' She waved a hand generally to include the spacious lawns and shrubbery, the paddock with her two ponies, and the comfortable house.

'And when your father died, Brian became one of the signatories on your account?'

'How . . . how did you know?' she gasped.

'Ever wondered why he did that?' he countered.

'I know precisely why. He wanted to move money in and out, to keep an eye on things for me so that my money earned as much as it could,' she said with a lifting of her chin.

'A rather weak excuse. Money went out, but from the time that your father died, nothing went in. Haven't you examined your statements?'

A worrying thought nagged at the back of Jemma's brain. Once, she'd questioned the fact that she was in the red, she remembered, but Brian had said that he was holding her money safely on a high interest account and would return it with bonuses. She'd taken a year off, before going to university, so that she could work in Spain to improve that language, which she was studying among others, and she still had her finals to take next term. Brian had talked about bonds, and shares, and how she'd have a lump sum to start her on her way, and she hadn't really listened, only thought at the time that it had seemed all so sensible and helpful . . . Jemma drew in her breath. Now Vasari was making even her suspicious! How easily doubts crept in, fed with lies by a master of deception.

'I don't know how you've discovered this information,' she said coldly, 'but I can imagine you have your well-paid spies. You're adding the art of listening at keyholes to your list of crimes, are you?' Her eyes flashed with scorn.

Vittorio gazed down on her proud, unrelenting face impassively. 'By being a signatory, Brian had the right to withdraw any sums he chose, and he exercised that right to its limit and beyond, far beyond. I'm surprised you haven't heard from an irate bank manager. Maybe he's expecting you to inherit money from the estate. I'm afraid he's going to be disappointed.'

Her brain whirled. She hadn't written any cheques for a couple of weeks. Her rent had been paid in advance, she hadn't wanted any new clothes, and the sum she'd drawn for day-to-day living expenses had been large enough to tide her over. She wouldn't know how badly she was overdrawn now. But what Vasari was suggesting was preposterous! 'I don't believe you!' she said, incredulously.

'I am telling you,' he growled, 'that your brother was not the man you thought he was.'

Her eyes blazed for a brief, split second before her hand cracked across his face. The Count flinched, there was a slight whitening around his nostrils, and Jemma slowly dropped her hand in fear as his chest expanded and his lips parted to reveal clenched, white teeth, bared in anger. Then she remembered that *she* was in the right, that he'd insulted her dead brother, and raised her hand to strike him again as the white-hot fury burned in her brain.

But he was too quick for her, this time. His strong hand snaked out, catching her wrist and drawing her to him in fury. Her body thudded against his and she smelt the maleness of him, felt his hard strength.

'You always hated him, didn't you?' she cried frantically. 'Resented the way he saw through you, and that he dared to fall in love with Luisa!'

'Listen to me,' he said tightly, staring into her defiant eyes, his fingers digging into her flesh. 'I don't like telling you these things, but how else am I to make you understand? Jemma . . .'

His mouth had altered. His voice had altered. The way he held his body was different. For, with her body crushed against his, Jemma had gradually begun to savour the subtle scent that emanated from his body, and she had trembled visibly. She knew what it was like to be enfolded in his arms and kissed by those lips which were curving so desirably.

She stiffened at his blatant sexuality. A groan of self-disgust was wrenched from her body, and pain etched lines into her lovely face.

'Still sex-mad. So beautiful, so tantalising,' he said scornfully.

Her heart hammering, she raised confused cornflower eyes to his, her brows drawing together in a puzzled frown.

'No!' she snapped, arching her back to escape.

'Superb. The most accomplished temptress I have ever met,' growled Vittorio. 'One day I may be hungry enough to accept what you are offering.'

Jemma tried to jerk away in denial, but his hand whipped around her back and pressed her ruthlessly against the length of his body, his other hand curving around the nape of her slender neck. Heat surged into her veins and she came alive for the first time in years, revelling in the exhilaration that fired through her, the way his eyes lit up in bright blue flames, how her skin seemed to hum and every part of her body lived just for him and his touch.

With a savage oath, Vittorio caught her chin brutally

and roughly angled her face, his thumb lightly trailing over her parted lips along their outline, over the fleshy swell.

'Get your filthy hands off me!' hissed Jemma, astonished at the way her body was betraying her need for him. Furiously she pushed against the immovable wall of his chest, but he merely responded with a sinister smile.

'I have you, Jemma. I have you just where I want you.'

She paused. Vasari was taking his revenge on the Mortimer family for the loss of his cousin in the only way he knew how: by degrading her, moulding her body to his and driving everything from her mind but the throb of her blood and the shaming melt of her loins. Thus she was in his power. He was in control of her, able to dictate any terms he cared to make. How she despised him!

She tried to twist her head away, but the relentless grip on her chin forced it back. 'What have you thought, over all these years, Jemma, when a man has held you in his arms?' he asked, his voice unusually harsh. 'Did you compare him to me? Or was I soon lost in the succession of lovers who shared your bed? Did you have lovers?'

'Of course I did,' she lied coolly.

'Of course,' he muttered. 'Well? *Did* you ever think of that moment our lips first found each other?'

She remembered. God, how she remembered! Somehow she had to get out of this situation and the hell-hole he was digging for her. 'Not that I can recall. At the time, I was quite impressed at how well you kissed,' she drawled. 'Such expertise! I often wondered whether it was your real profession. As a gigolo, you'd make a fortune.'

Vasari's gasp of rage was terrifying, but her words had caused him to release her. Jemma calmly adjusted the lie of her jacket and smoothed the crumpled skirt to give her time to assume the right expression of indifference.

'I must be very careful how I play this game.' His growl hid a dark undercurrent of violence. 'You tend to break all the rules. I forget you have no breeding. I am so used to respecting women and treating them politely that it is hard to break the habit of a lifetime and treat you as you deserve. *Dunque* . . . I am released from the normal courtesies of gentlemanly behaviour. I won't apologise for my boldness in holding you so intimately. Few red-blooded men could stand so close to you and resist your charms. And my blood runs red and hot, Jemma.' His inscrutable eyes glittered down on her.

'Really?' she drawled. 'I thought your blood was cold and blue.'

The haughty pride of centuries gave an air of remoteness to his bearing. 'I am pleased to see you for what you are, Jemma,' he said in diamond-hard tones. 'Although I find I can't actually speak the word that describes you.'

'You do have such a clever way of insulting people while retaining a cloak of respectability,' she said scathingly.

'Thank you,' he said with a small, ironic bow.

Murderous hatred still lurked close to the surface. She must tread carefully. Still, the momentary danger had passed. Now she hated him more than ever for finding the weakness in her armour. He'd caught her off guard;

it wouldn't happen again.

'Jemma!' Christobel's voice called from the patio, and Jemma turned to see that she was beckoning. 'People are leaving,' she shouted.

'*Allora,* don't forget, leave the bookmakers to me,' urged Vittorio.

She threw him a look of pure scorn and walked away haughtily.

The guests left, while Vittorio talked to the bookie and then Brian's accountant. Jemma was dimly aware of papers being exchanged, and then her unwelcome visitors had nodded to her genially and roared away in their Bentleys.

'You know,' said Christobel, coming up to her, 'you were mistaken about that man.' She nodded to the Count, lurking in the background. 'He's really rather nice, and such a gentleman. Are you sure you've got your facts right?'

'Gentleman? He's a swine! He fools everybody like that,' said Jemma bitterly. 'Look, we lived through his treachery and lies, remember? He's cruel, and I have no regard for insensitive men and neither should you! The Italian family bond is very, very close and very important, I know that much, and Vasari deliberately broke that bond, preventing Luisa from ever seeing her kinfolk or Italy again. I'll never forgive him for that, never!'

'Oh, Jem! I didn't know you felt that strongly. Do you want Charles and me to stay? The Count said he had some business to discuss with you,' said Christobel.

'No,' she said, wearily. 'I can handle him. When the going gets tough, all I need to do is to be sarcastic. He hates anything that hurts his dignity. I'll be all right. I need to win this one on my own. Thanks for all your support.'

She saw Christobel and Charles to the door and stood there for a moment, steeling her mind to the forthcoming conflict.

Vasari was waiting for her in the drawing-room and he rose as she walked in, a slim, lovely woman whose face was a cold, expressionless mask.

Ignoring him, she began to collect some glasses and line them up on one of the trays left by the maids, who were bustling around, clearing up.

'That is not your job,' said the Count. 'I am paying others to do that.'

'*You* are paying?' she snapped. 'Forget it, Vasari. You'll impress no one here. There's nobody to pass on your lies.'

'They are not lies. I think you ought to listen to what I have to say.'

'I've had enough for one day,' she said, irritably. 'I can't expect you have any compassion but, like it or not, I'm unable to cope with you after everything that's happened. Mrs Parks! Will you see this . . . person . . . out?' Her voice held a quavering note of desperation in its appeal.

'To his room, do you mean, dear?' asked Mrs Parks, looking puzzled.

'Room? No! He's leaving. Point him towards the front door, and help him through it if you have to,' said Jemma through her teeth.

'But I've made up a bed for him . . .' said Mrs Parks.

Jemma dropped a glass from her nerveless fingers and the housekeeper became occupied with organising someone to mop up the dregs of wine that had spilled.

'There is a lot to discuss, Jemma,' said Vasari sternly.

'You can't keep on evading the moment. The last thing I want to do is talk to you in a civilised way, but it is necessary.'

'No, no, *no!*' she yelled, clenching her fists and emphasising every word with them. 'Go! Out of my sight! I never want to see you again, never, do you hear?' Her voice trembled and a suspicion of tears was welling up behind her eyes. 'Show some small crumb of pity!'

Vittorio was waving away Mrs Parks and pushing Jemma into a deep armchair. 'Sit there. Calm down.' He stared at her as she shook with anger. She was on the edge of breaking down completely. 'Pity?' he asked harshly. 'You expect me to show you sympathy?'

Her eyes widened at the tight set of his jaw. The man was loathsome. He had no idea of the emotional wringing she had been through over the last couple of days. Or if he did, he didn't care. Only his vendetta raged relentlessly in his blond head.

'I expect nothing from you,' she said with icy calm. 'Only arrogance, deceit and carnality.' In a deliberately indifferent gesture, she crossed her long, slim legs and met his cynical eyes with a challenging stare.

'*Madonna!* I have a good mind to pick you up and take you to Italy this minute!' he muttered.

'Italy? That's the last place I'd go,' she said with distaste.

'You'll come,' he said menacingly. 'You will have no choice.'

A cold shiver rippled down her spine at his certainty. Bluff. Brave words that would amount to nothing. He had no hold over her.

'However,' he said, his mouth curving into a sardonic smile, 'I think you're in no fit state to talk sensibly. It would be no good to speak now, much as I'd like to get this unpleasant business over with and return home. You'd be unable to listen rationally.'

'I'll never be in a state to listen rationally to you!' she cried fervently.

'You must be, tomorrow. I can give you no more time than that. Yet for now, I think you need to lie down. Before you do, have a look at this.' He took a thick document from his inside pocket.

Jemma tried to read it, but the words jumped around in a blur. 'I can't,' she whispered, holding it out to him.

'You have to, if you are to understand why I am entitled to stay here the night,' he said grimly, coming over to her side. Immediately she was aware again of the fragrance that always pervaded his skin and how it had once clung to her body. Pains tore raggedly through her, pains she hadn't experienced for years. 'It says that I own this house,' he said in a low, husky tone.

She walked unsteadily to the window, staring at the wisteria that dropped its lilac plumes in a delicate framework. The clink of glasses and the clatter of plates as they were removed irritated her beyond belief. She must get a grip on herself.

She opened the document slowly and looked at the name of the property and the name of the owner. Il Conte Vittorio Romano de Vasari di Montevecchio. Then the date. Two weeks ago. She even recognised the accountant's signature beneath Brian's: it was the same signature that had appeared on the paper authorising Brian to use her account . . . She sank to the window-seat, her legs like jelly. What was going on? she moaned to herself. There must be some perfectly good explanation. But not now, not *now*. She passed a cold and shaking hand over her face.

'Go upstairs, Jemma,' said Vittorio sternly. 'I will see you in the morning. Try to rest.'

Obedient for once, she walked up the stairs like a zombie, undressed, and took a long, long bath, shutting out everything but the feel of the perfumed water and the sensation of relaxation as the warmth seeped into her bones. Mechanically she dried herself on a huge, fluffy white towel and slipped on a delicate peach night-dress, wondering how she could sleep, knowing that somewhere in the house lay the man who had killed the two people she loved most in the world.

In a valiant attempt to put Vasari completely out of her mind, she lay down on the black satin counterpane, cradling her head against the glossy, sinful pillows. She flicked the switch on her bedside console. Soft, dreamy music floated over her, soothing her splintered brain a little. The exhaustion of the terrible hours washed over her and the wonderful release of sleep took over.

CHAPTER THREE

SLEEP replenished Jemma's strength. With a little luck and a great deal of control, she should be able to handle the Count and any new revelations he cared to make. Brian's secret vice had been a shock: she'd known he was a bit of a rapscallion, but not that he was innately irresponsible. It was obvious that she'd have a lot of sorting out to do. She sighed. At least it would occupy her mind.

And she'd better get on with it. Opening her huge wall cupboards, she scanned the racks of clothes for something intimidating and perfect, something that she felt good in. Eventually her glance landed on a stark black jersey dress by Saint Laurent, its severity emphasised by the high, draped throat and long, clinging sleeves. The subtle cut wouldn't be lost on Vasari. When she had finished preparing herself, she presented an image of a remote, icy woman, whose ash-blonde hair lay neatly against her skull, coiling at the back into a complicated, gleaming twist.

Whatever he threw at her, she'd be ready. The light of battle glinted in Jemma's eyes. She drew herself erect and sauntered into the breakfast room to see Vasari, darkly elegant in a sharply tailored black suit and burgundy waistcoat, returning from a stroll in the frosty garden. She poured herself some orange juice and coffee as he joined her, determination in every line of his forbidding body.

'I'm going to talk,' he said, his face hard and uncompromising, 'and you're going to sit there and listen until I have finished the whole sordid story. Then I'll tell you what you have to do, and I can go home.'

Jemma reined in her temper. 'Well,' she said in a bored tone. 'Get on with it.'

'I had thought to spare you one or two details,' he said coldly. 'But I don't think I'll bother. You're hard enough to take what I have to say.' His long fingers fiddled idly with a spoon and Jemma prepared herself for his words. 'As I mentioned yesterday, Brian was a heavy gambler. I discovered that when I first met him.'

'Oh? How?' she asked languidly, her eyebrows raised to express disbelief.

He shrugged his expensively tailored shoulders. 'Personal observation. Later this was confirmed by gossip, banks, credit companies, angry clients, my Intermediaries . . .'

'Who?'

He made an irritated exclamation. 'It sounds as if you know as little about your father's business as Brian.'

'Just cut out the smart comments and explain,' she snapped.

'Your father had two or three people in Italy who showed prospective clients over property, acting as middle men. We call them Intermediaries. Unfortunately your brother saw fit to neglect them and forget to pay their expenses.'

Jemma stifled a curse. 'I said . . .!'

'I know, and I'm not commenting, I'm telling you the the facts,' he said harshly. 'Those men had families to support and Brian kept promising them payment in full. So they trustingly continued to work for him and thus lost many opportunities to find a secure job.'

'You only put their side of it. Maybe they were inefficient. Maybe Brian realised that they were an unnecessary indulgence,' she defended, not letting him see that Brian's callousness had upset her deeply. She'd make sure the men were reinstated immediately—but she wasn't giving Vasari the satisfaction of knowing her mind.

'I might have expected such a heartless remark from you. Intermediaries are essential. Italian property laws are complicated and someone is needed to work between the buyer and the seller, bringing them both to a contractual stage without evoking forfeit clauses. No wonder nothing has been sold for over a year without them.'

Jemma made a mental note to check on that. No doubt he was making wild exaggerations. 'It all sounds unnecessarily complicated,' she said, turning to the attack. 'Bureaucratic. Typically Italian.'

'It *is* complicated,' he agreed sardonically. 'The middle man is part of Italian business life, from selling a chicken to buying a Michelangelo. *Dunque,* in view of Brian's failure to make any money, and the way he was spending it, I wasn't very surprised when he asked to meet me in London.'

'What?' Jemma banged down her cup of coffee. 'Brian hated you! You really expect me to . . .'

'Just listen,' he snapped, uncharacteristically. 'He was desperate. He told me about his gambling losses and that he'd withdrawn everything from your account to help cover them. That's when I learned how he'd become a signatory,' he explained. 'He asked me to save him from prison by buying all his assets, giving him the option to buy back in the future.'

'All . . . you own everything?' she gasped in horror.

'I was doing your brother a favour. I was the only one he could turn to, the only person he dared to tell. He said I owed him this, for Luisa's sake,' he said bitterly.

'Well, you did!' declared Jemma, her eyes cold chips of blue glass, her brain whirling. What were the implications? If he owned the house, the business . . . Her stomach rolled. He had her in the palm of his hand.

'I couldn't allow Luisa's husband to go to jail,' he said, ignoring her outburst. 'Anyway, it seems you have inherited more debts since that time. Look at these papers.'

She found it impossible to keep her lips from trembling as she leafed through the damning evidence. Oh, God! she thought. Was that why there had been so little laughter in the house recently? Her hatred for the Count increased.

'You caused this,' she said quietly.

'I made your brother gamble?' He laughed unpleasantly and laid his arms on the table, leaning forwards with a frown. Jemma's eyes dropped to the half-inch of perfectly shot cuff and the gold lions rampant on the massive links. 'Perhaps you would tell me how I managed to force him into casinos and clip joints, how I persuaded him to subsidise the bookies' cruises to the West Indies!'

'Don't be ridiculous. You drove him to it. By being such a bastard about Brian and Luisa's marriage, you destroyed part of her,' she said levelly, speaking clearly and making every word count. 'From the first day she came back here after the honeymoon, I knew she wasn't completely happy. I'd walk into a room and find her crying. She refused to say why; I know it was your doing! You tore her from her homeland, from her roots, and the people she loved. She was bound to be in despair sometimes, however loving Brian was. She shed a lot of tears over you, Count Vasari!'

The naked distress in his face shocked her. She saw him fighting for control, as he swallowed and then bit his lip hard with those sharp, white teeth of his; his lashes lowered to hide the expression in his eyes. 'Luisa? Tears?' He could obviously say no more. And then she knew for sure, with a sickening judder of her body, that Brian was right, that the Count had been furious, not only for his family pride in that Luisa had married a nobody, but because he had genuinely expected to marry his cousin himself. He had more guts maybe than she'd originally thought. By banning Luisa from contact with the Vasaris he was also denying himself something he wanted very badly. The man had a will of iron. And stubborn? God, he was stubborn!

'You loved her, didn't you?' she said quietly.

A huge fist thumped down on the table, making the cup jump and rattle in its saucer. 'Of *course* I loved her!' he yelled, pushing back his chair with such force that it turned over. Heedless of this, he began to stride up and down, like a caged lion, a lion who ran an angry hand through his mane and whose eyes and teeth and tensed, erupting body threatened danger.

Jemma's heart had already been broken. Hearing Vittorio announce his feelings for Luisa so openly and so cruelly tore open her wounds and left them bleeding again.

'So you *were* acting out of spite. And are you sorry for what happened?' she asked bitterly.

'Yes, yes, *yes!* I am sorry we ever came here. I would

be at peace with myself and Luisa would be alive if it wasn't for you and your brother.'

'They died because of you!' she said furiously, jumping up. He really didn't understand what had happened, even now. 'Luisa was so unhappy, and Brian tried to make it up to her. He gave her extravagant presents and parties. That's where his money went. He adored Luisa. And she adored him,' she added, cruelly, wanting to hurt him. 'They died because he'd decided to buy her a sports car, and she wanted to drive it, even though the conditions were wet and slippery. If he hadn't been trying to compensate for her lack of family life, they'd both be alive. It was you who killed them!'

'No! Damn you, don't say that! It's not true!'

'It is! And for that reason I hate you! Now will you leave?' She drew herself up to her proud height. How she kept her face a blank she did not know. Pride, probably.

He was staring miserably out of the window, a wild pulse hammering in his temple and a dark, driven look on his face.

'I can't leave yet. You are my responsibility now,' he said in a remote voice. 'I am the only family you have.'

'Family!' She laughed hysterically. 'I have as much wish to be part of your family as I have to be part of a band of cut-throats.'

'You are dependent on me. I intend to sell this house immediately. You'll vacate it by the end of the week,' he said in a remorseless tone.

'What about the house staff? And my ponies . . .'

'I'll take care of them all. They won't suffer.'

Her world was being turned upside down. Oh, Brian, she cried silently, how could you *do* this to me? To put her in this terrible man's debt . . . She pulled herself together.

'I'll get a job. I'll work till I drop and pay you back, every penny,' she vowed savagely.

'Don't bother. You'd go to your grave a pauper. You know roughly the value of the house. Add to that the business at an estimated five million and the thirty thousand pounds of debts outstanding . . .'

Her eyes narrowed. 'If you gave Brian five million pounds, then where has it all gone?' she cried, thinking that she'd trapped him in a lie.

'I said he *asked* me to buy his assets. I didn't say that's what I did. I paid off his debts, gave him and Luisa a small income and held the business and house as surety. I gave Brian nothing.'

'You cheating bastard!' she breathed, enjoying the sight of him flinching.

'There's no point in giving a gambler a fortune. I had to make Brian work for his living. It appears he didn't. Pack your things. I'll take everything belonging to Luisa,' he said relentlessly.

'What am I going to do?' she breathed. 'I'll be on the streets!'

Her skin prickled in alarm as his insolent eyes made a leisured tour of her body. 'Not for long,' he said in a patronising tone. 'Not with a body and morals like yours.'

'You do know how to hate, don't you?' she scathed, turning away. Where she was to go, she didn't know. Perhaps Christobel might take pity on her . . .

'Wait!' His voice cracked like a whip. 'I haven't finished with you yet.'

'Go on,' she said, turning with resignation. 'Pile it on.'

'You'd like to sit your finals, I imagine.'

'There's not much chance of that now, is there?' she said listlessly. All that work wasted! She had no other talents, apart from her languages.

'Why not? You're studying at Newcastle, I believe?'

'Is there anything about me you don't know?' she asked sarcastically.

'Where do you live? In Hall?'

'No. I rent a flat.'

'I'm prepared to advance you a sum sufficient to keep you there until you have sat your exams. On a condition.' There was a quiet menace in his eyes.

'I am not going to bed with you!' she spat out.

His mocking eyes raked her lovely body in the svelte black draped dress. 'That, if you will forgive me for saying so, is of considerable relief to me.'

'You . . .!' She became speechless with rage—a rage directed at herself, for blurting out her sexual fear of him so openly.

'Say it if you wish,' he said languidly. 'I am becoming used to the barbarous behaviour of your family. After your finals, you will work for me.'

Jemma's mouth dropped open. 'You're joking!'

'Not at all. You will travel to Italy to act as an Intermediary, and I will appoint a temporary manager of the business over here. You speak good Italian and would be perfect to show English clients over the properties. That body of yours will combine well with your cool manner in selling. When you know the job a little better, then I think you would be capable of taking over the management yourself. Think about it, Jemma. It will be a good career. And soon you could be making your own decisions, handling the business just as your father did.'

'Except he owned it! I won't do it!' she cried passionately.

Vasari fixed her with hard eyes. 'If you prove to be difficult, I'll have you slapped in jail faster than you can blink.'

'Why bother to keep me out, if you hate me so much?' she snapped.

'I told you. Family. Oh, don't imagine it was my idea, Jemma. My mother sent me. She said I must do everything I could to make sure there was no scandal attached to the Vasaris. It is a matter of honour that we keep you from the guttter.'

'I ought to slap your face for saying that!' she seethed, her hands curling into claws.

'You look like a wild tigress, ready to tear it to pieces,' he murmured.

She turned her head quickly to avoid the strange light that had come into his eyes. His sensuality was overwhelming. She felt its effect on her: cruel and angry flames of desire chasing through her body.

'Well?' he demanded.

'Your terms are marginally preferable to prison,' she said coldly. 'But if the job includes being touched by you then you can forget it. I'd rather be locked up and the key thrown away!'

By the time Jemma landed at Leonardo da Vinci airport in Rome at the beginning of summer, she was a different woman. Even more slender and fragile than before, her face had taken on a haunting, ethereal look, as though her translucent skin was paper-thin and she was living in another world.

Her performance in the exams had been appalling, and it was unlikely that she would gain her degree after all. When Vittorio had left, everything had collapsed around her. There was no longer the need to be strong and fight, and gradually she slipped into a deep trough of depression. The shock of Brian's and Luisa's deaths became real, and the misery of her situation and the dependence on Vittorio combined to make her feel a helpless pawn in life's game.

Instead of her spacious, sunny flat, she'd been forced by the stinginess of the Count's allowance to move into a tiny, depressing bedsitter in a basement. Christobel and Charles had no idea she was in trouble, and thought she was selling the house to escape painful memories. They would have helped her, but she couldn't bear the idea of being in more debt.

Used to spending lavishly, eating expensively and enjoying frequent visits to the theatre, she felt as though she'd been living in a cultural desert for the last few months, and her brain seemed dulled as a result.

There was little to keep her in England. The house had been sold, and the staff well catered for. Even Mrs Parks was singing the wretched Vasari man's praises, at the comfortable income he was providing for her. He was wealthy enough to pay off everyone, but evil enough to make her his slave, she thought morosely.

Resolved to show the Vasari tribe that she was equal to them, and to rebuild her father's business, she worked hard to study the history and tourist attractions of Tuscany and Umbria where the majority of the business was centred. She would more than earn her way. She'd climb to a position of security and then find a way to snub the arrogant Count.

Glamorous and aloof in a white linen suit and wide-brimmed fine straw hat with a black scarf tied around the crown, she waited at the previously arranged pick-up point for the Count's chauffeur. He was late. Her dainty feet, shod in strappy white sandals of an impossible height—to intimidate the Count—tapped impatiently on the pavement. Already it was mid-morning and the sun was very, very hot, rising past the nineties. She considered returning to the shaded canopy, and just as she made up her mind to do so, two *carabinieri* stopped her and spoke in Italian.

'*Signorina,* you will please excuse this apparent discourtesy of speaking to you when we have not yet been introduced, but we believe you to be the Miss Mortimer, yes?'

Hiding a smile at his flowery Italian, she answered him in his own language. 'I am Miss Mortimer. What do you want of me?'

'Regretfully, that which I want of you, *signorina,* I am prevented from disclosing to you because of your gentility and my official capacity. Therefore, it is with sorrow that I must pass on my message and leave you.'

She did smile at that. Italians were so good at giving compliments without causing offence, and she felt better immediately! It was rather nice to be admired.

'I hear,' continued the man, 'that the driver for *Il Conte de Vasari* has had a small argument with a large lorry. He has broken the leg.'

'Oh! That's awful! Poor man. I'd better take a train, then,' said Jemma, worrying about the cost.

'No, no, *Il Conte* will arrive. He is in Civitavecchia and when he finishes his visit there he will collect you at the Piazza Navona, perhaps this will be at five o'clock this afternoon.'

'Five . . .' She bit back her irritation. 'Thank you,' she said politely.

'Not at all, *signorina*. Goodbye, we hope you will enjoy Rome.'

Jemma smiled and nodded her thanks, then the reality of the situation dawned on her. She looked with annoyance at her outfit. She'd been expecting to step straight into a car and be swept up the Autostrada de Sole to Vasari's palace. After hours in the blazing sun, she'd look like a rag when he picked her up. That wasn't how she wanted him to see her!

She went over to the taxi rank and haggled in the most bored manner she could summon up, till the driver halved his fare and had settled her in the comfortable back seat. The traffic was horrendous and it took over an hour to reach the centre of Rome, where she left her bags in one of their Day Hotels and changed into flat shoes and a thin cotton dress to do a little sightseeing.

It was nearing five when she finally made her way to a café in the Piazza Navona, claimed by the Romans to be the most beautiful square in the world. There, dressed elegantly again, and with her luggage safely under the eye of the *patrone,* she relaxed at a table over a leisurely iced lemon drink, watching the Romans, and being watched, and propositioned, in return. As her eyes drifted over Bernini's stunning Fountain of the Four Rivers, she saw the Count, striding across the pedestrianised *piazza,* scattering pigeons as he walked. He must have had a long day, working in the heat, yet looked perfectly cool and as well-groomed as ever, in a blue-grey suit with matching shoes and tie. The fluid strength of his body, as he walked, his confidence and apparent ignorance of the admiring glances, made him look overpoweringly male. Jemma had forgotten what an impact he always made on her. It disturbed her every time.

Infuriatingly, her heart began to thud and she felt very nervous. There was no getting away from the fact that he epitomised male virility in the way he moved with that haughty bearing and natural grace. It *was* rather like watching a feral creature stalking his prey, she thought idly, staying seated. Let him find her. She was damned if she'd leap up and attract his attention by waving like some excited child.

The pavement cafés were densely packed, for this was where the elegant Romans came to see and be seen. His eyes flickered over the throng, occasionally acknowledging friends, occasionally pausing to smile and re-examine a beautiful woman and linger over her inviting glance.

Jemma's throat dried as his scanning eyes swept nearer, and she sipped her drink, pretending to look the other way. Then she became conscious of his well-manicured fingertips resting on the table in front of her.

'Good afternoon, Jemma. How are you?' he enquired politely.

'Hello.'

He paused at her unenthusiastic reply and then continued. 'I apologise for the delay—it was unavoidable. I hope you have enjoyed your time in Rome.' He waited for her comment, which was not forthcoming. She was just looking at him steadily, with no expression on her face at all. His blue eyes darkened. 'Perhaps we might leave immediately. I am triple-parked. You have luggage?'

She turned and beckoned the waiter, calling for her things. Digging into her wallet to pay the exorbitant bill, she noticed a little cynically that he made no move to pay it for her. Apparently he felt no need to act like a gentleman any longer, and that suited her! Except that he'd made her come to this expensive place and pay a ridiculous price for her drink. She rose, wondering how on earth the Count was planning on shifting her two heavy cases across the *piazza*. It would surely be beneath his dignity to carry them himself? To her surprise, he lifted them as if they weighed nothing, and she remembered those rippling muscles. She ran her tongue over dry lips.

'It's not far,' said Vasari. 'The next *corso.*'

Jemma remained silent, aware that he was examining her with an insulting thoroughness. It unnerved her. She hoped he wasn't thinking that he might take advantage of her, now she was a stranger in his country and at his mercy. Did they have such things as the *droit de seigneur* in Italy? she thought wildly.

'Here.'

Four members of the police force were prowling around his car, and Jemma felt a secret delight as he calmly opened the boot and stowed away her luggage. But then, when she had been escorted to the passenger seat, he set about explaining his predicament to the police and miraculously they were all smiles and bows. Being a count obviously paid off, especially if you could talk your way out of anything, with your practised, silver tongue.

'You'll find out why we call this the Infernal City, rather than the Eternal City, Jemma,' he said as they drove away. 'I'm afraid the traffic will be impossible. It will take some hours before we arrive at Montevecchio.'

She shrugged elegantly. 'It makes no difference to me. I'm perfectly relaxed.' In reality, the thought of spending some hours in this metal box with a sexy count sent shivers up her spine.

'That is true. You look very cool. Too thin, but extremely elegant. I had expected to find you tired and wilting after spending the day in Rome's summer heat.'

He swerved to avoid a suicidal pedestrian and exchanged courteous insults.

'I kept to the shade. And I showered in an *Alberghi Diurni.*' She'd also spent a great deal of money by doing so, and in having lunch. Her wallet was a lot slimmer than a few hours ago, because she hadn't bargained on a day out in Rome.

'How clever of you. I regret the inconvenience. You look even more like a model than when I last saw you, Jemma,' he said, his eyes roving boldly over her body, and gleaming when she tensed.

'Keep your eyes to yourself, and don't think you own me just because you are giving me a job,' she said tightly. 'I will work for my money, you can be sure of that.'

'What money?' he murmured.

She turned to him in shock. 'My pay! My wages!'

For a moment, he was unable to answer, as he negotiated the pavement. Count Vittorio de Vasari was an impatient driver, like all Italians. He didn't wait politely to overtake; if there was a gap, he slid through it! Jemma's heart was in her mouth as he judged the distance between the offending stalled car and a pavement display. He sounded his horn loudly and forced his way back into the traffic stream. No one turned a hair. Such behaviour was perfectly normal, almost demanded of a red-blooded Italian male, it seemed. Last time Jemma had been in Rome, she had used the buses and metro. She'd never been driven through the rush hour by a maniac before.

'Your wages? Yes, you will be paid. Though some deductions will be made. *Idiota!*'

'What deductions?' she persisted, inwardly seething, as he gesticulated expressively at a group of drivers in the middle of a crossroads, conducting a theatrical argument. A nearby policeman had been halted on his way to the problem by a lovely young girl who was unconcernedly threading her way through the traffic, swaying seductively, followed not only by the policeman's eyes, but by a chorus of admiration.

Jemma's irritation deepened. She was in a sea of chauvinism! Macho drivers, ogling women. Why hadn't she noticed this before? It explained a lot about the arrogant Count and the cavalier way he treated her.

'The deductions will be the first payments for the debts I have paid for you and the allowance you used up while you were in your final term,' he said coolly.

'But . . . you never said . . .'

'Surely you didn't think I was keeping you without expecting something in return?' he murmured softly.

He was deliberately building sexual tension, Jemma thought angrily. What did she have to give him but her body? 'You're not going to . . .' she gulped, unable to put her fear into words. The fever climbed within her. His eyes were lingering on her mouth, dropping to her breasts . . . She pressed her knees together to crush the flickering flames. 'I said I'd do this job if you didn't touch me,' she said shakily.

'I remember.' His liquid voice flowed to join the melting heat in her loins. 'I can't recall agreeing to your terms, though. Still relaxed, are you?' he enquired silkily

Jemma quickly dropped her shoulders and stretched out her slender legs, steeling herself to accept his indolent gaze as it ran up their golden length. 'Tell me, Count Vasari,' she said quietly, 'what does a moral country like this think of rape?'

He chuckled. 'It's difficult to say. Either Italian men are so persuasive that it never happens, or women never bring such cases to court.'

'I always was a trendsetter,' she said.

Vittorio's flashing grin annoyed her. He was supposed to be warned off, not amused!

'You're quite a woman,' he said in admiration. 'I'm going to enjoy our work together. Did I tell you that you wouldn't be paid until the end of the month? I hope you have enough cash to manage till then.'

She gathered her wits together. 'I—I don't have much money at the moment. I'll need some soon—certainly before the end of the month.'

'Then you'll have to be nice to me, won't you?' he smiled nastily.

Drat him! He was making her feel like a poor relation, begging for a crust! And what did he mean by *nice?* 'You swine . . .'

'Not a good start,' he grinned. 'Have you any idea how little you are going to have left each month?'

'I don't believe even you can keep me penniless,' she said, her voice like splintered ice.

'I can keep you how I like,' he said softly. 'I virtually own you, Jemma.'

'Like hell you do,' she muttered.

'Like hell, I do,' he agreed annoyingly. 'I often thought the Devil was as much a prisoner as the people he enslaved. Still, it gives me some pleasure to know that you suffer.'

'That's a very immature attitude,' she said scathingly.

'I believe in justice,' he countered. 'I intend to make sure you repay every penny of your debt. Every single penny.'

'You can't do that to me,' she said firmly. 'I owe so much that it would tie me to you and your family for years.'

'Yes.'

Jemma stared at his smug face in fury.

'Ah, some life in those eyes at last.' He smiled mockingly.

'Damn you! Damn, damn, damn you to hell!' she yelled.

'Please. Don't soil your beautiful lips with such words. I don't like women to swear,' he said quietly.

'I do whatever I please,' she glared.

'I think not,' he said, his lips sensually full. 'You do as *I* please.'

Jemma was unnerved by the sexual threat. He was right. He did have her in his power. She was his vassal. Through the temper-fraying traffic jams, which meant that it took nearly two hours to crawl out of Rome, Jemma sat in a stiff silence, refusing to speak to the hateful man beside her. She thought he began to drive provocatively in a deliberate attempt to wring some word from her, but she kept her lips tightly closed, even though he snaked through the tortuous traffic with frightening arrogance, paying scant attention to happily infuriated drivers who howled gently barbed insults at him. After a while, she realised that this was a game that they all played and that he was, in fact, superbly skilled, his eyes glancing from left to right and into the rear-view mirror all the time, using his quick reflexes to stay out of serious trouble.

Jemma felt all her nerve-endings becoming finely tuned to his every move. There was definitely something very sexy about the way Vittorio drove his car, murmuring, coaxing, muttering, and she was ashamed of the way her eyes strayed to the shifting movements of his legs stretching out to the pedals, the way he caressed the steering wheel and gear-stick. She bit her lip hard and stared out of her window.

Once on the *autostrada,* the powerful car throbbed and purred, smoothly swallowing the miles. In the distance she could see high mountains. It would be a long time before they arrived, time in which she could get a grip on herself and make plans. The Count thought he could do what he liked with her, did he? She'd see about that! She had no intention of crawling for favours and licking the boots of some petty feudal lord!

CHAPTER FOUR

THE last thing Jemma remembered was the crescent moon rising above the mountains, and being unable to control her head as it grew heavier and heavier. Then she was dreaming, stupidly, romantically, of being in Vittorio's strong arms, snuggling into the curve of his warm shoulder and being content at last. All the bad things that had happened to separate them, and arouse such an intense hatred for each other, were swept away. So it was with dreams.

She felt his firm mouth fasten hungrily on hers and opened up to him like a parched flower, impatiently thrusting aside his jacket, tugging at the soft shirt till it was free of his waistband and she could run her hands around his lean waist to the warmth of his spine. A thrill spun through her head as her fingertips touched the satin smoothness of his skin and began to explore each bone in gently circling movements.

He was murmuring beautiful Italian words of love, of tenderness. In her elation she moaned with relief that in her dream she could say what she wanted.

'Make love to me,' she mumbled out loud.

Her words broke the spell; suddenly it was all too real. At his shuddering response and deepening kiss, she opened her eyes dazedly and discovered it wasn't a dream at all.

Alerted by her stiffening body, Vittorio raised his lashes, a puzzled look filling his slumbrous eyes. Jemma

77

rammed the heel of her hands into his shoulders and his warm body lifted away immediately.

'Don't touch me! *Don't . . . touch . . . me!* I thought—I didn't know it was *you!*' she spat contemptuously.

In a violent movement, he flung himself into the driver's seat, his breath rasping between gritted teeth, his golden head thrown back on the seat, exposing the sharp angle of his jaw and the tanned column of his neck. Still half-way between sleep and wakefulness, Jemma's gaze fastened on his throat with a pagan longing. It was such an even honey colour, and so flawless, that she had to occupy her hands, pushing feebly at her hair, otherwise they'd be reaching out to stroke the perfection of his vulnerable skin.

His head rolled in her direction, his eyes narrowed and the haughty nose and mouth curling in scorn as he followed her unnecessary preening. A long hiss of angry breath was released and his chest deflated—but expanded again, and Jemma could tell how difficult he was finding it to hold back his temper.

The amber light of dawn flooded the landscape with an unearthly glow, gilding the stubby blond hairs on Vittorio's chin. A whole night must have passed! Her jacket had been removed and laid across her body, her seat was now inclined horizontally. It looked as though she had slept here right through the night, with Vittorio beside her. The thought of his sultry eyes watching as she slept without any of her usual defences filled her with dismay. She struggled upright, neatening her clothes.

'Who did you think I was?' asked Vittorio through clenched teeth.

'What? Oh . . .' She reached down to her shoes, hooking a finger under the strap that ran around her heel so that they fitted comfortably. She'd been wearing them when she fell asleep. He must have bent down and eased off the ankle strap, then held each foot as he slipped off the shoe. Jemma's face flushed to think of his long, slender fingers curving around the high arch of her foot. It was such an intimate thing to do. In order to hide her temporary confusion, she made sure her head was down as she sat back in the seat again, so that her hair curtained her face. Then she realised. It shouldn't be doing that at all, it ought to be pinned neatly in place.

'You unravelled my hair!' she gasped, whirling around to glare at him.

'Very slowly,' he said. 'You frowned every time you leaned back on that complicated arrangement. It must have been very uncomfortable.' The tip of his tongue moistened his lips and Jemma stared, mesmerised by it. 'I found the process of loosening . . .' He paused, and Jemma could see that he wasn't only referring to her hair. There was a knowing look in his eyes, damn him! ' . . . Well, it was a delicate and laborious business. But I managed it in the end. I always do.'

He certainly did, she thought sourly! Just as well he didn't know how much he'd loosened her up. She loathed herself for the spiralling coils that clutched her treacherous body.

'You've got a nerve,' she complained.

'Several. All humming away,' he mocked.

'I don't like their tune.'

'Then I'll try another one. I have quite a repertoire,' he murmured.

'You self-satisfied, smug . . .'

'This is being nice to me?' he enquired with a lift of his eyebrow.

'It's impossible to be nice to you,' she said with irritation. 'Where's my hat?'

'Try harder,' he said, twisting his body to reach a long arm into the back and handing the hat to her.

She had pressed against the car door, away from the nearness of his body. 'I want to do my hair. You'll have to wait while I put it up again. It takes ages,' she said icily.

'Yes, the tumbled look doesn't go with that elegant suit,' he said. 'Leave it for now. I'll take you somewhere you can do it properly.'

He fastened his top two buttons and began to push his shirt into his waistband. When he unsnapped the fastener on the waistband of his trousers, she looked away quickly, listening to his movements as shame washed over her. *She'd* crumpled that once-immaculate shirt in her impatient hands, pushed it up and felt the splendour of his muscular back. A sharp pang reminded her of the sheer strength of his body beneath her hands. She'd better get used to the fact that Vittorio was a potent sexual force as far as she was concerned and learn to deal with it. It was patently obvious that he considered she was fair game and needed to prove his masculinity by pawing her. What she had to do was to make sure that her head ruled her body at all times. She gave a sigh. Easier said than done!

He'd opened his door and stepped out to stretch his long legs. The rising sun turned his hair into white fire and highlighted the pronounced bone-structure of his face. Jemma jumped out of the car and slammed the door, rubbing her arms in the fresh dawn air. They were in a fertile valley of orchards and lush vineyards, surrounded by the isolated hills that characterised Umbria. When she'd first seen pictures of the landscape, she'd been reminded of the lawn at home, studded one morning with molehills. She lifted her head in an attitude of listening. Very faintly, from one of the distant villages, came the sound of church bells, and as she stood, the warmth of the sun gained strength and the air began to hum with insect life.

Yet none of this calmed her. Vittorio had parked beside the road under a line of poplars in an area so quiet and remote that she tensed, realising how alone they were.

'Shall we go?' enquired Vittorio. 'Or would you like a few more moments to dream of your lover?'

'I'd need more than moments to remember his love-making,' she lied sweetly. 'Don't judge other men by your quick satisfaction.'

He stopped, his hand on the car door, and Jemma froze as his hard eyes raked her body. 'Careful with your challenges to my masculinity. It would give me the utmost pleasure to spend a whole day arousing you until you begged me to take you,' he growled. 'Then I might, or might not, allow you to discover how much it takes to satisfy me.'

'Heavens, I've met Superman,' she tossed at him, as she slid into the car.

He eased himself into the driving seat, a slight smile playing about his lips. 'Don't tempt me to shake that remarkable courage of yours,' he said. 'And remember, you are in my debt.'

'Maybe,' she said. 'But that doesn't give you the right

to grab me when I'm sleeping. What on earth did you think you were doing?'

'Responding,' he drawled.

'You mean that in my sleep I invited you to kiss me?' she scorned.

'Indirectly. As we slept, your head dropped to my shoulder and somehow my arm crept around you. I was only half awake when I woke to your warmth and began to kiss you, and you know the rest. It was a reflex action, it's easily done,' he sneered, at her incredulous face. 'You joined in for a while, till you fully woke.'

Colour seeped into her skin. He must have been woken frequently by amorous women to get that kind of instant knee-jerk response in his sleep! 'Yes, well, as I said, I thought you were someone else,' she explained, hoping to save her pride.

She was pinned back violently to the horizontal seat as Vittorio slammed her down again, his angry, glittering eyes a few inches from hers. She recoiled from the physical threat as his body hovered over hers, the intimidating male strength filling her with anger.

'Who?' he demanded tightly.

'None of your business!' she defied, still warmly liquid inside from his kisses. She hated herself for her malleability as far as he was concerned. It was almost indecent the way her body called out to him.

'It *is* my business. You're part of the Vasari family,' he muttered, 'and cannot get involved with trash. How many times have you made love to this man, that when you stir in your sleep you imagine he is kissing you?'

'You're hurting my shoulders. You're bruising me!' she protested.

'Answer!' he barked.

'Go to hell!'

'I'm already there!'

Jemma quailed at the low-pitched growl. Vittorio had taken Luisa's death very badly. He must have loved her a great deal to be still mourning with such passion that those words had been wrenched from the very depths of his grieving soul. What a waste of a man's love, that it had been given to someone who never wanted it. Vittorio was very dangerous. A man who imagined himself in hell would have nothing to lose. 'If I wanted to, I could . . .' He paused, as though contemplating some cruelty.

'You could what?' she cried, jealous anger lending her courage. She'd loved sweet Luisa, but envied her capacity to fire Vittorio's emotions.

'I could force you to tell me,' he said menacingly, flexing his body.

Her azure eyes challenged that threat. 'Try! You'd love that, wouldn't you, to inflict pain on me? It would release some of that guilty anger about Luisa that's raging inside you. Well, go ahead! Hurt me if you want to! But I'll fight you with everything I've got, and you'll have some explaining to do to your mother when she sees your scarred face!'

Hot with aggression, she held his eyes fearlessly, saw them darken, saw his expression become first sensual and then ferocious. 'I don't want you to talk about Luisa,' he said tightly.

'I'll bet you don't,' she snapped. 'You can't bear to face the fact that your love for her wasn't big enough to let her have what she wanted.'

'You don't understand. You know nothing of my feelings.'

'Feelings?' she cried incredulously. *'You? Feelings?'*

His fingers tightened cruelly on her arms. 'That was a mistake, Jemma,' he said in a terrifyingly soft voice. 'An Italian male cannot resist so many challenges. And you've been issuing them like a frustrated medieval knight who hasn't thrown down a gauntlet in years. I will show you that I have feelings.'

'I—I m-m-meant . . .'

The cold stillness of his face, the remote look in his eyes made Jemma's blood freeze. It had been stupid to get so angry. She could only win her battles if she stayed calm. Vittorio was the only man who had the capacity to infuriate her like this, and every time she let him get past her protective indifference, he won further ground.

'I know what you meant,' he grated. 'Since you hate me to touch you, since you hate my kisses, then that is how I will punish you.'

'Oh, God! No!' she moaned, unable to summon up a wall of composure as his hands idly caressed the fragile bones of her shoulders. There was no one around; the road was empty, the countryside uninhabited. She was at his mercy and would have to fight him every inch of the way. For all her bravado, she feared his sexuality, because she was well aware that there would be a moment when her body began to betray her and strain for his caress. And then he would have won, not only the battle, but the war. She would surrender herself to a merciless avenger.

'Yes, Jemma. And the joke is that I will make you enjoy your punishment,' he said cynically, his mouth descending.

Jemma tightened her lips against the hard, unrelenting pressure, denying him any pleasure in his physical mastery of her. He merely laughed harshly, his eyes blazing with fire, and dragged her roughly against his body, so that she could feel his hard, tensed contours and knew that he was enjoying the sensation of her firm young body as it quivered angrily against his.

Her head twisted from side to side, and she managed to wrench her mouth away, but then his lips were savaging her throat, and his hands roamed over her back uninhibitedly, insulting it with their intimacy. She wriggled in his grasp, and heard his low, chuckling laugh of pleasure as their hips moved together.

He wanted her. She was terrified of his arousal and the practised way he had managed to trap her hands and prevent her from attacking him. What had started out as a short, sharp lesson was turning into a potential rape. Sick with fear, she shuddered violently.

'Not enjoying your punishment?' he asked, his eyes like slits.

'No!'

'Then I suggest you don't provoke me again,' he snapped.

Her body thumped to the soft leather seat again as he abandoned her, abruptly. Shaking, but glad to be unscathed, Jemma scrambled up. He'd called a halt—for now. How much more was he going to torment her like this? How many times would she be subjected to his scorn before he took her?

That was the worst part—to know that he despised her and had every intention of treating her like a whore. Maybe she ought to try and explain what had happened at that party. Maybe he'd respect her if he knew she was a virgin and innocent of men. For a moment her heart leapt at the thought, and then she saw his tight-lipped expression and knew he'd never believe her.

His hand pressed a lever and the back of the seat came up to meet her rigid spine. The engine roared. 'Wait a minute,' she said coldly. 'I don't think I can take much more of your attitude. If you're going to behave like that every time I see you, I want to go back to Rome.'

He cut the engine and smiled unpleasantly. 'You prefer prison to my arms?'

Jemma stared ahead blindly. If he ever knew that her distress stemmed from her hatred of herself, at the helpless arousal of her body by the man who had caused her brother's death, then his revenge would be sweet. But she could never tell him, because he'd make sure that his seduction was complete, and his triumph would be all the greater.

He gave a short laugh. 'Such a dilemma! You must hate me very much. You'll suffer no more attacks like that,' he said in a low tone. 'None. We've both had our punishment. It's over. It was a mistake.'

'Both? What do you mean?'

'Never mind,' he growled. 'Shall we just say that I find I regret touching you?'

'Oh.' Jemma didn't know what to make of that. Did he regret touching a woman he imagined to have few morals, or did he regret not behaving like a gentleman? Whatever the reason, from the look on his face it seemed it was the end of any intimacy between them. She was glad.

Hot, pricking tears filled her eyes and she quickly averted her head, only to find it being turned by Vittorio's hand.

'Don't cry!' he snapped sharply.

'I'm *not!*' she raged.

He let out his breath harshly. Jemma didn't move, letting her limpid eyes meet his. She only had to look at him, she thought bitterly, to feel her heart stretch out to him. And if his eyes looked at her with that pooling warmth much longer, she'd be lifting her mouth to his and making a complete fool of herself.

'This has become intolerable,' he muttered, voicing her thoughts, his lips too tender, too close. 'We must both try to control our feelings. Jemma, this has begun very badly. I am appalled by the things that have happened this morning. You make me act so irrationally . . .' He passed a hand over his golden head.

'I make *you* . . .!' Jemma was speechless. That was typical of him, to turn it into her fault!

'We never used to anger each other, Jemma.' The slow warmth of his voice seeped into her brain, softening it.

'No,' she said, a little less heatedly. 'But too much has happened for us to be friends again.'

'Friends?' he said, barely audible. 'I thought we were more than that.'

She gave a brief shrug of her shoulders to counteract the memory. 'People deceive each other,' she said.

'Yes, I learnt that the hard way,' he muttered. 'Look, we both have a job to do and it'll be easier if we're not fighting all the time. I must teach you how to be an Intermediary, and you need to listen and learn. I know I've acted badly and there are reasons, many reasons why. You know some of them. But we must work together. The sooner you learn the business, the sooner you can go home and we can both be left in peace. You'd like that, wouldn't you?'

'Yes,' said Jemma, blocking out the bitter wash of

emptiness.

'I thought you might,' he said grimly. 'So, we'll try to be polite to each other. And before my mother we must be courteous.'

Oh, yes, thought Jemma, that's what all this has been leading up to. He was afraid that she'd let drop a few home truths. The Marchesa must never know what a bastard he was. Then it occurred to her that all she had to do, if Vittorio forgot himself again, was to threaten to tell his mother all about him: his sexual escapades in London, and his treatment of her. That should guarantee her protection.

'*Dunque,*' he continued, 'we will forget we are enemies. Yes?'

Relief flooded over her, but she didn't answer for a while, letting him sweat. Finally, quite composed, she nodded.

'Thank you,' he said, to her surprise. 'Then you accept my apology?'

He held out his hand and she looked at it in astonishment. Her eyes flicked up to his face suspiciously, but he looked sincere. In fact, she thought she detected a tinge of shame in his expression. She took his hand and felt its warm dryness as his fingers gripped hers for a brief moment before dropping away in an embarrassed silence.

'Well,' he said lightly, 'as they say in cowboy movies, let's go! Everyone will be wondering what has happened to us. I certainly didn't intend to fall asleep so soon after you did. That's the penalty of not going to bed the night before.'

Jemma's brief relaxing of her antagonism tightened up again. She felt her mouth curl in disgust as the car purred into throbbing life. So that was what he'd been doing in Civitavecchia! Living it up away from Mamma's watchful eyes! Aware of his curious glance, she stared stonily at the scenery.

'We're coming up to Rieti,' he said quietly. 'I suggest we stop there for breakfast and to freshen up. I can ring home and say we're on our way.'

Jemma was glad to stop at a hotel that was equipped with a powder room so that she could comfortably recreate her well-groomed appearance. Breakfast would be a relatively civilised affair, too. Normally, Italians breakfasted in the dozens of small bars scattered throughout towns and cities, taking their coffee and pastries standing at a counter. She preferred to sit down to a table and be less rushed.

Vittorio had been shaved by the hotel barber and the process must have relaxed him, for he behaved as if the incident in the car had never occurred. He was charming, attentive and rather fun—as he had been in the old days. For a while Jemma kept up a cool façade but, with Vittorio commenting on their fellow diners with much wit and perception, she was unable to prevent laughter from bubbling out.

Perhaps he was embarrassed at his own lapses. If so, she'd play along and keep the atmosphere light. After all, they would be thrown together over the next few months, and if she could establish a polite, easy relationship then her feelings need never surface.

He told her a story about a bandit who captured a fat and ailing abbot, and unwittingly restored the abbot to health with a diet of bread and wine, thus earning himself a full pardon for his sins. He told her of the servant who went ahead of his master, sampling the wines of Italy, only to be so enamoured of the dry white wine of Montefiascone that he remained in the vineyard, rapturously drinking himself to death.

As he spoke, embellishing the stories with rich descriptions, her heart chilled to watch him, and to listen to his deep, sun-warmed voice. She would never escape him. The lazy smile, the expressive gestures, his stunning colouring—all combined with his charismatic personality to pull her more surely into his clutches. She knew he was doing it all deliberately, and hardened her heart.

They drove on, out of the city and into the flowing Umbrian hills over a bridge that spanned a deep gorge between two massive volcanic outcrops. A valley of golden sunflowers turned their huge, soft faces to the sun, and Jemma thought that if she stayed there long enough she would see them moving, in their endeavour to soak up the best of the rays.

'You can take in the view from here,' said Vittorio, stopping the car on a hairpin bend in complete disregard for any other traffic—although Jemma had to admit that they'd seen nothing on the road for a long time.

All around rose steep hills, covered in chestnut and ilex woods. The limpid light intensified both the colours and outlines of the landscape, sharpening the silver of the olive trees in the valley below and the deep pink of the city of Assisi, spreading like an ancient fan on the slopes of Mount Subasio.

'We have a couple of properties in Assisi,' he said, his eyes resting thoughtfully on her enchanted face. 'So we will be visiting the town.'

'Oh, yes.' She'd forgotten she was supposed to be here on business. Her face fell. She doubted that he'd give her much time for sightseeing. She'd be too busy giving him his pound of flesh. Not too literally, she thought wryly. She didn't fancy a nightly struggle outside her bedroom door.

'How are the Vasaris involved in the business?' she asked.

'Through owning property. We seem to breed cattle less prolifically now, and have been selling off some of the farming estates. My father met yours at the Italian Cultural Institute in Belgrave Square—an exhibition of costume, I believe—and discovered a mutual need for each other. He became our agent. He was enthusiastic, efficient and delightful.'

Jemma smiled wistfully. 'Yes, he was. Though I didn't see him much, apart from when he entertained business contacts at home.'

'It was his great regret,' said Vittorio, his eyes scanning her face. 'When he visited us in Italy he often talked of you. But he couldn't stop working. When he did, he said that all he felt was pain.'

'Because of Mother?' Jemma was astonished that her father should open up to Vittorio.

'It was an all-consuming love that he had for her,' he said quietly. 'Love like that is a blessing and a curse. There is always a danger, in being raised to the heights of rapture, that you have further to fall. I know this. I understand. Your father found it particularly difficult to be with you because you were so like your mother. I heard of your devotion to him and your brother, how even as a little girl you took it on yourself to care for them and be the woman of the house.'

'Father seemed so helpless,' said Jemma in a low voice. 'My strong, courageous father, suddenly bewildered and dazed. I had to do something. Looking back, I must have seemed rather precocious to his guests when I welcomed them with such gravity: a little girl in pigtails and ankle socks!'

'They were charmed. You don't remember my father, do you?' murmured Vittorio. Jemma shook her head. So many had come to the house, and she'd been preoccupied with pleasing her father. 'He could speak of nothing but you when he returned: how you tried to anticipate everyone's needs, how you watched your father constantly, making sure he wasn't too tired, hot, cold . . . It touched my father deeply. Especially the pain on your father's face when he looked at you, as you solemnly handed around the drinks and canapés. It was obvious to everyone that the small womanly gestures you made had been unconsciously learnt from your mother, and that they brought him some bitter-sweet memories.'

'I never knew.' Her face softened. Poor Father. He must have felt the same pain and longing that she did when she thought of Vittorio.

'That doesn't surprise me. You English are very secretive about your passions,' said Vittorio drily. 'As I discovered to my cost.'

'Please don't,' she said, remembering how Brian and Luisa's affection for each other had come as a great shock to her, too.

'I'm sorry. I've lived with bitterness for so long. I, too, prefer to work non-stop. We'll begin tomorrow.'

'That suits me fine.' The sooner she started, the sooner she'd learn the job and be able to get back home. 'Surely all the property on the books doesn't belong to you?' she asked.

'It did at first. A farming estate holds many buildings which convert into homes, and there were many estates. Now our friends also dispose of property through us. And my mother has begun to release some of her lands. You see, when she marries, a woman retains her own possessions and her husband doesn't interfere in her business affairs. Mother has her own farms and villas, her own summer and ski retreats.'

'I approve of women retaining their property,' said Jemma firmly.

He grinned. 'I'm sure. Then you'll also approve of the house in Assisi that's built into the ramparts. It belonged to my great-aunt's lover. They met there for years, till her death.'

'How tragic,' said Jemma, surprised at the revelation. The Vasari women weren't *that* pure, then!

'Not really,' he smiled. 'She was seventy-nine.' He laughed at her astonished face. 'A widow. She refused to give up her independence. Our women have always been difficult to pin down even for a moment, let alone capture. Anyway, you'll be able to see it soon. It's a beautiful house, full of character, and there's a definite atmosphere of happiness about it. The stone is the colour of old gold and there's a balcony, crowded with pots of flowers, that looks over the valley.'

'It's still lived in, then?'

'No longer. A neighbour looks after it. You'll find that in Italy local people will automatically keep watch on property that is empty. So don't be surprised if you are unlocking a door and someone turns up, asking questions. They're being protective. I believe you have something like that in your country.'

'Oh, yes. Neighbourhood Watch.' An image of her

lovely home flashed before her eyes—the pool, the cool, fragrant gardens—and she suddenly felt very homesick. Meeting Vittorio, the drive and her humiliating response to him, his terrible charm, and the surging memories of her father, made her want to be back in England where she knew the rules and understood the people. Tears welled into her eyes and furiously she looked away, blinking to keep them back and biting her lip till she felt blood.

Vittorio gave a sharp exclamation and leaned forwards to study her face. Jemma was too proud to hide from him.

'You miss your own home?' he asked softly.

Miserably she nodded. 'I don't want your pity,' she breathed, squeezing her eyes shut. 'I don't want your kindness.' If he showed her tenderness at that moment, she knew she'd bawl like a baby.

A soft lawn handkerchief brushed her cheeks, then she felt a warm mouth enclose each eyelid, somehow taking away the desire to cry. Slowly he drew his thumb over her lower lip; his mouth kissed along a rivulet of tears and lightly sucked the salty blood. The sweetly sensitive gesture stabbed cruelly at her heart.

'You've had a strange life, Jemma,' he murmured. 'With your father shut in his own world, no responsible person to teach you the difference between right and wrong.'

'I had Brian.'

He frowned. 'Yes.' There was a pause. 'Well, shall we go on? My mother is on pins waiting for us. She's looking forward to meeting you. She is so nervous!'

'Nervous?' Jemma forgot her unhappiness. What on earth had the Marchesa to be nervous about? She was the one who dreaded meeting Vittorio's mother!

'Very much so.' His mouth curved delightfully over his white teeth. 'She is anxious that you will think our house is beautiful and that you will love her.'

'Love her?'

'My dear Jemma, if you keep repeating things I say, Mother will think our hearts beat together,' he teased, laughing again to see her blush. 'Of course she wishes you to love her. You are family. Remember that, Jemma. We are all you have.'

It gave her a comforting feeling, somehow, that she did have someone of her own after all. It was odd, because it ought to unnerve her, being connected with the Vasaris, since she had none of their noble background. Once, she had rejected any suggestion that she had anyone else in the world. Now it appeared she needed that security. As if to confirm their relationship and his brotherly protection, Vittorio kept one arm around her slender shoulders as he drove onwards, giving her an occasional reassuring squeeze. Despite her misgivings, this was better than the hostility between them.

They turned off the main road and the valley ahead was suddenly filled with vines, strung like garlands between mulberry trees. Jemma remembered reading something about peasants having to plant the trees to supply the silk industry in Florence, to the north.

'There! Montevecchio!' said Vittorio proudly, with a flourish of his hand.

In the bright sunlight, against a backdrop of distant blue mountains, the thousand-foot hill rose directly from the valley bottom, the toast-coloured houses cascading down the slopes like an ochre river, as though they'd been sliding down for centuries. Jemma knew that most of the town was unchanged since medieval times, but it was different discovering that as a fact in a reference book and seeing it, before your eyes. A pleasurable feeling came over her, and it was as if she was coming home. She felt her nervous anxiety smooth away as her face softened and relaxed.

'It looks so peaceful, like a Sleeping Beauty town,' she said with a smile.

'It hasn't always been so innocent. Over two thousand years ago it was an Etruscan stronghold. The streets have run with blood—especially in the Borgias' time. But now it lies with the silence of centuries, as you say. You will love it, I am sure. I hope so, for it will be your home while you are in Italy.'

They snaked up the zigzag road that led to the town, with panoramas at every turn, and drove through the main gate. Vittorio skidded cheerfully around the fountain in the middle of the *piazza,* acknowledging the shouted greetings from people in the small *trattoria* on one side. Then they were entering an archway, dominated by a carving of two lions.

'They're like your cuff-links!' she exclaimed in surprise.

He threw her a grin. 'We earned the right to one lion from King Richard I. The second is the symbol of Florence, and it was the result of marriage into the Medici family.'

'A love story?' asked Jemma dreamily, seeing golden-haired women, in rich brocades, being courted by handsome Medici princes.

'Hardly. The Vasaris didn't get to be wealthy by marrying for love.'

She was silent, the light dying from her eyes. Perhaps that was why he was so heartless. He knew that he was destined to marry some rich or well-born woman and provide her with children to carry on the line. She could almost feel sympathy for him, because he would one day make a loveless marriage for the sake of the dynasty. Brian had taken so much away from him.

The car was crawling along the drive to the *palazzo* through an avenue of dark green, pencil-shaped cypress tress.

'Be careful when you are able to drive along here, Jemma,' warned Vittorio. 'There are often children playing in the grounds. We always seem to have relatives staying.'

More cousins being groomed to be his bride? Jemma was about to comment, when the house came into view. It was a huge square building in the Romanesque style, the colour of tobacco leaves, the smooth paint peeling here and there with an air of crumbling gentility. A baroque fountain graced the semi-circular drive in front of the house, sun-sparkled water gushing from the mouths of roaring lions.

As Vittorio accelerated the last hundred yards or so, he pressed continually on the horn and people began to scurry from the door and run down the long flight of steps in Carrera marble that led to the front door.

He handed her out politely, but she could see that he was holding back an exuberance that had nothing to do with her, and he turned, to be enveloped in the arms of a huge lady, dressed entirely in long, flowing, black crêpe. She hugged him and kissed him as though he'd been away for weeks, rather than days, and Jemma groaned inside. Mamma doted on him. He'd be unbearable from now on—even worse than before!

After he had been fondly greeted by a bevy of servants, he turned to Jemma, his face beautiful in its happy excitement and an unusual warmth in his eyes. The depth of her feeling for him dismayed her. Like this, stripped of his harsh arrogance, he seemed the loving and humane man she had fallen in love with. *Seemed*, she told herself.

'Well?' he demanded, placing his hands on his hips and cocking his head on one side. 'What do you think of the *palazzo?*'

'It looks very grand,' she said without emotion.

'Grand? Nonsense. It's just a home. Now, meet Anna. She was my wet nurse and the second woman in my life.'

'Your . . .!' Jemma found herself drawn into the fat lady's ample bosom, which was extraordinarily powerfully corseted, and kisses were deposited on her cheeks.

Still elated, Vittorio rescued her and introduced her to the rest of the servants, who seemed to be fascinated by her ash-coloured hair. Jemma was stunned. She'd known that many Italians had a maid, even relatively ordinary people, since everyone had a young cousin or distant relative who had fallen on hard times and was happy to work for her keep, but the Vasaris had a stableful of employees! And as for the wet nurse . . .!

'So,' said Vittorio, ignoring the car and all their possessions scattered in it. Presumably everyone would run around after him, collecting and sorting, parking and depositing everything in their right places. No wonder he was a bit high-handed, with this life-style! 'Come and meet the family.' He placed a friendly arm around her shoulders and escorted her up the stairs. 'It's wonderful to be home. It's almost worth while going away, just for the pleasure of the return. And this time, I bring back a beautiful woman to adorn the house. I must confess, I've been looking forward to seeing you in this setting.'

'Back to your habitual flattery, I see,' said Jemma in a slightly caustic tone. It was almost worth taunting him, if it would remove that look of joy on his face. It made him far too appealing.

'You are beautiful enough to adorn anywhere, without trying. I must teach you how to differentiate between flattery and a compliment from the heart,' he said evenly.

Disconcerted as she was, it was a moment before Jemma became aware of her surroundings. They were in a huge entrance hall, which stretched up to a vaulted ceiling, decorated with frescoes. Slender columns formed an arcade all the way around the hall, each column topped by a lion. Marble statues stood in niches and fine bronzes graced Venetian console tables.

She'd been right, the house was grand.

'Perugino,' he said casually, as her eyes scanned the scenes of court life on the walls.

Jemma shot him a quick glance. Perugino was one of the most famous painters of his day. She only had time to nervously straighten her linen jacket before two men and a woman emerged from enormous double doors.

'Welcome! Welcome to the Palazzo de Vasari di Montevecchio, my dear. And, it is now your home, of course. Ah, but you must be so tired! I do hope my son has not taken you sightseeing. He has not explained why you are so late.'

A tall, very elegant white-haired lady was walking

across the marble floor, her heels clacking almost in time with her words. So that was where Vittorio got his mouth, thought Jemma, seeing the Marchesa's beautiful smile!

Jemma panicked, wondering what to do, how to greet her, as Vittorio pushed her forwards. 'Jemma Mortimer, Mother,' he said, and to Jemma's ears it sounded as if he was proud of her. His hand in the small of her back propelled her towards the ramrod-straight lady, whose simple pastel dress was up to date and probably priceless, judging by the way it flattered her slim figure. Sensing her uncertainty, the Marchesa placed her hands in Jemma's and kissed her on both cheeks, releasing a waft of delicate fragrances.

'If he has tired you out I will be very angry with him. Now we are talking English for some time, on Vittoro's orders,' she said, in her soft, gentle voice. 'He is such a bully, of course, and we don't always take any notice of him. Men can be such an irritation sometimes, can't they? But this time, he is right. We must make you feel at home, even with our funny accents and funny sentences. I do hope you don't obey Vittorio always?'

Jemma gazed solemnly at her amused face and then her peal of laughter rang out across the vast hall. 'Certainly not,' she gurgled.

'Excellent! Good morning, my dearest heart,' she said to Vittorio, who kissed his mother's hand and then her cheeks, three times.

'Mother, it's marvellous to be back.' He smiled indulgently.

'Of course, of course it is. And so,' she said firmly, turning back to Jemma, 'these ill-mannered young men whose eyes will admire your beauty, until Vittorio roars

at them, are my sons. This is Gianluca, and this is
Enrico.'

Forcing back her giggles, Jemma offered her hand to
be kissed by the two young men, both of whom had
Vittorio's startling Crusader colouring. The Marchesa
was hilarious! It might be rather fun here, after all.

'Miss Mortimer, I am overwhelmed. Vittorio said
your beauty was incomparable, but he omitted to
mention the warmth of your smile. Only the watchful
presence of my mother prevents me from falling to my
knees at your beauty,' murmured Enrico.

'And the smart crease in your trousers,' observed
Gianluca.

Jemma laughed with the others at Enrico's hurt
expression.

'Jemma is English, Rico, and will probably always
laugh at your compliments, so I suggest you tone them
down a little,' said the Marchesa drily. 'By the way,
Vivi, why are you so late? I remember now, I was going
to be angry with you. We expected you last night.'

'I telephoned,' protested Vittorio, and Jemma
realised who the Marchesa had been speaking to. It
amused her to hear his nickname. It made him less
intimidating.

'You left messages, you mean,' said his mother
sternly. 'With servants. That is not good enough.'

'You were all out, Mother,' said Vittorio patiently.

'What was it that kept you from bringing Jemma
back here yesterday?'

There was a ring of steel in her tone. Jemma
wondered how much she clashed with her arrogant son,
whose mouth had become very determined indeed. And
she wondered how good he was at lying to his mother.

'I didn't arrive in Rome till after five. It took hours to escape the city. Jemma fell asleep and I felt drowsy too, so I thought I'd better pull over. You wouldn't want me sleeping at the wheel, would you?' His eyes smiled at his mother. 'I was so tired, I slept through the night. You know, I've hardly paused for breath over the last few days. We stopped to freshen up and took our time. I took it easy for Jemma's sake, so she did not arrive tired and irritable.'

'The poor girl slept in the car? With *you?*' The Marchesa's face was a picture.

'The Ferrari is very comfortable,' said Vittorio tightly. 'Really, you're making a fuss.'

'I hope it did not prove to be too comfortable, Vivi,' she said sternly. 'What will Jemma think of you? Did you ask her if she wanted to spend the night in a car? Did you ask her if she was insulted? Did . . .?'

'*Marchesa,*' broke in Jemma quietly, 'I fell asleep. So soundly asleep that I didn't wake until the morning. I think it would have been dangerous for Vittorio to drive on if he was so tired.'

'Hmm. You are being very kind. Vivi works too hard, you know. Ever since . . .'

'Mother!' Vittorio's rapped-out reproof startled them all. He drew white teeth over his lower lip in an obvious effort at control, continuing in carefully modulated tones, 'Perhaps Jemma can be shown her room while you tell me how Carlo's broken leg is healing. Come down when you are ready, Jemma, and we will have lunch. I expect we will be on the terrace, through the archway, but shout if you get lost and I am sure that a thousand willing men will come running to assist you.'

She smiled faintly at his exaggeration and followed a

maid up the ornate stairs, eyeing the faded tapestries
and family portraits that hung on the landing. The
golden hair and the Vasari mouth were a dominant
feature.

Vittorio had firmly guided his mother through the
arch and his brothers had followed, giving her a couple
of surreptitious glances that she pretended not to notice.
Vittorio might defer to his mother in some things, but it
was obvious that he ruled the house. She hoped she'd be
able to prevent him from ruling her—though his
attitude had relaxed remarkably since arriving at the
palazzo.

Her bedroom overlooked a cloistered inner courtyard, its honey-coloured walls covered in scrambling
white roses. Dotted around the courtyard were huge
terracotta pots, like those on her carved wooden
balcony, filled with brightly blooming geraniums and
tiny orange trees. She leaned on the balustrade, while
the maid unpacked her clothes. The peace of the old
palazzo settled over her. Jemma stayed for a few
minutes, breathing in the scented air, then washed her
hands, checked her appearance and went to find the
family.

Soon she felt perfectly at ease. Under the shade of an
ancient vine, they sipped Frascati and gossiped while
Vittorio's extravagant gifts to his mother and brothers
were unpacked and exclaimed over. Her sense of being
his bonded slave disappeared entirely, as it was made
plain that she would be one of the family. His brothers
seemed to think she was the most beautiful woman they
had ever seen, though she was sure their admiration
wasn't entirely sincere! But it was amusing to see how
much their eagerness to talk to her annoyed Vittorio,
and that he watched them like a hawk. Perhaps he was

afraid that she'd seduce them!

Lunch was a vast affair: *antipasti,* then pasta, then casseroled turkey with olives, potatoes and *fagioli,* followed by almond tart and plenty of cheese. They ate outside, on a terrace framed by cascading jasmine. Jemma was perfectly willing to comply with the ritual of the siesta after lunch, especially as she had drunk quite a lot of wine with her meal.

A servant followed each member of the family, closing the dark green wooden shutters so the room was bathed in a cool half-light. Jemma slept.

In the late afternoon, the Marchesa commandeered Vittorio to discuss business, much to his anoyance, infuriating him further by delegating Gianluca and Enrico to show Jemma the layout of the house and garden. She was quite happy with them. They seemed a little prone to make suggestive remarks, cleverly hidden by rambling sentences, but compared with Vittorio they were easy to handle, so she had an enjoyable time.

The formality of dinner was a different matter. Jemma realised that she had been underdressed at every stage of the day, but especially that evening. The Marchesa was resplendent in a long evening gown of peach taffeta and jewellery worth a king's ransom. The attentive, dinner-jacketed men, the grandeur of her surroundings and the daunting array of shining silver and twinkling glass on the table all conspired to make Jemma very aware that what she'd once considered wealth was pocket money to the Vasari family.

She stared at the candlelit table and the Venetian gilt-wood chairs bitterly. She really was the poor relation. And Brian's debts could have been paid from the sale of the huge chandelier in Venetian glass. If the Vasaris were so keen to prevent scandal, why hadn't they just settled the debts, sent a sharp letter of rebuke, and made sure she was working for her living? Why bother to re-open old wounds and drag her over here? Her throat contracted at the brooding look in Vittorio's face, and her tongue slicked over her lips to moisten them. She retracted it quickly when his teeth snagged at his own lower lip, and his hot eyes met hers. Of course. He was determined to possess her. She felt the colour drain from her face.

'Now, Vivi,' said the Marchesa in concerned tones, 'you are not to work Jemma too hard. See how delicate she is! My dear,' she said, confidentially to Jemma, 'he is, I fear, brutal to the women who work for him. Every time I go to his office, there isone crying.'

'Don't exaggerate, Mother,' smiled Vittorio.

'Often we have to swim into the building,' explained Gianluca wickedly teasing his brother.

'If you have *ever* seen any women crying in my office, it's because they want to be paid like men but not be spoken to like men,' said Vittorio drily.

'Or because they're in love with you,' grinned Gianluca.

Vittorio shrugged. 'I can't do anything about that.'

'You have the same trouble, Jemma, yes?' murmured Enrico. 'Many men in love with you?' He smiled at her over his glass.

'I've no idea,' she said quietly. 'I'm not particularly interested.'

'What a relief!' said the Marchesa. 'I am so tired of falling over women who adore Vivi. So boring. At last, my son, someone who does not find you attractive.'

Jemma smiled. 'Oh, I do think he's attractive,' she said pleasantly. 'I like pretty things, like all women.' She lowered her eyes, and felt Vittorio stiffen as the rest of his family chuckled. 'But a man must be much more than that to interest me. I haven't yet found one who can offer all the qualities I demand.'

'That, Jemma,' said Vittorio, his ruffled composure apparently smoothed over, 'was a very Italian insult. *Brava*. And something of a challenge.'

His last sentence sounded threatening, but his face was innocent. However, she noticed that he found it difficult to smile at the outrageous remarks made by his mother, who was scattering intimate details of her family with rare abandon through the conversation. He brooded, his eyes almost a midnight-blue in the candle-light, obviously disliking the easy friendship Jemma had formed with his brothers, and even his mother kept shooting him frowning looks, in an effort to make him remember his manners.

That night, with nightingales singing sweetly outside to a background chorus of cicadas, Jemma went to bed happier than she had been for some time. She had established a warm relationship with the delightful Marchesa, and had begun to fit into her surroundings. The only blot on the horizon was Vittorio. She had an uncomfortable feeling that the truce between them was only temporary, and that one day he'd stop hiding behind his Latin charm and wreak his vengeance.

CHAPTER FIVE

JEMMA struggled out of a heavy sleep to discover a maid in her room, cheerfully drawing the heavy brocade curtains. The shutters banged open, pale gold sun shafted on to the bed, and Jemma's sleep-laden eyes focused first on the canopy of her four-poster bed, threaded with gold, then with growing disbelief at the clock.

Six-fifteen! She flung an arm over her face with a groan. Apparently the slave-driving had begun. In the far reaches of her foggy mind she could hear the maid's cheery voice bidding her good morning and telling her that *Il Conte* expected her for breakfast at six-thirty. Despite the awesome summons, her still slumbering body refused to do more than stumble around in a muddled fashion as she tried to find her things in the unfamiliar surroundings. It was almost half an hour before she appeared in the intimate breakfast room overlooking a small brick terrace.

Vittorio, as usual, looked superb, even at this ungodly hour. Her drowsy eyes took in his casual elegance and wondered whether she was underdressed again. He had his back to her and was reaching for the coffee-pot. The dazzling white shirt stretched tautly as the muscles expanded and played beneath it, emphasising the narrowness of his waist. Jemma considered the ice-blue trousers and shoes, wishing she hadn't panicked when she saw the time and thrown on the first items that came to hand. A pair of jeans and a plain shirt, however clean and well pressed, didn't look as if they'd be right for an outing with the Count.

He looked impatiently at his watch and she took a deep breath, walking into the room briskly and trying to halt the sway of her hips in the close-fitting jeans. His eyes were everywhere, touching her body and making it tingle with awareness and she set her face in a brittle smile.

'Good morning, Vittorio.'

He stared at her expressionlessly for a moment, as she secretly smoothed her damp palms over her hips, his lashes dropping in a thick, concealing fringe, then flicking up coldly at her. Too late, she stopped trying to dry her palms; he'd noticed. With a dark frown, he turned back to his coffee and addressed her in a remote tone.

'This isn't a good start. We should be leaving at seven.'

'I'm sorry, I . . .'

'No excuses, please. And . . . I'm afraid you'll have to change your clothes.'

'Oh.' She'd been right. 'What am I supposed to wear for a trip into the outback?' she asked flippantly.

Vittorio turned cold blue eyes on her. 'When you are in my country, working for me—and particularly when you are out with me—you will dress with care. In a dress. I dislike seeing women in trousers.'

'I don't believe this!' she exclaimed, sitting down in astonishment.

'If you were going to work in England, would you wear jeans?' he asked, biting into a pastry savagely.

'If I was tramping about estates, I would.'

'Hmm. Remember you're a businesswoman now, not a language student, and will act accordingly. You have an image to project, Jemma. Many people will see you in the next few weeks who could be important to your future, and they'll judge you first on your appearance.'

'That sounds rather a shallow way to . . .'

'First impressions are important!' he snapped. 'If it looks as though you can't be bothered to dress well, then people will think you can't be bothered to attend to details. How can I claim to be your patron if you look like a child of the streets? And please put your hair up. It makes you look like a seductress, the way it keeps falling over your eyes.'

He resumed his breakfast as though everything was settled. Jemma sat and fumed. She'd left her hair down partly because she didn't have time to perfect her simple but time-consuming style, and partly because it wouldn't have looked right with the casual outfit.

'Besides,' he said, slanting a glance at her, 'you'll be far too hot in jeans, as the day progresses.'

He was right, rot him! Initially she'd felt a little chilled in the early morning air, but it was already warming up. Regally, she rose and strode away, regretting that her own sleepiness and lack of organisation had put her at a disadvantage. She'd make sure she laid out her clothes the night before in future.

'Is this suitable?' she asked, a little later.

His eyes flickered warily at her face, expecting to find sarcasm there, but she was innocent of that and only hoping to please. As he took in her short-sleeved navy dress that emphasised her tiny waist, those expressive eyes of his kindled and the examination became more languid, returning to the curves of her body and then rising mockingly to her face.

'Perfectly suitable.'

She'd been determined not to let him incite her to anger or desire, but already she felt a treacherous tremble in her body. Anger, she told herself. But she'd keep it in check. Suddenly not hungry, she forced herself to eat a sweet pastry and drink the fragrant coffee while Vittorio began to explain her duties.

'To begin with, I'll teach you how to take details of a property—the points to look out for, the amenities and so on. Later you'll meet some people who will be useful when you return to England. We'll work from seven in the morning until one, when we break for a long lunch and siesta. Then we continue working from three to eight. Today, as it is your first day, we will stop in time to have tea here. Mother has invited some of our relatives to meet you.'

Interesting; she was being drawn into the bosom of his family. Or perhaps she was being vetted. In any case, it reduced the amount of time she'd spend in his company. 'That sounds rather fun. Are they as nice as she is?' asked Jemma, with a smile.

His face softened. 'Almost,' he replied warmly. 'They're all very curious to meet you.'

'Why . . .' She bit her lip and tried to phrase the question delicately. 'Why is the Marchesa so nice to me and . . .'

'And I am not?' he finished for her quietly.

'Well, yes, after all, Luisa . . .'

'Please,' he said in a low voice. 'I'd rather we didn't talk about her. Not yet, anyway. All you have to know is that the rest of the family don't have the same feelings about you as I have.'

'I see.' That was plain enough. He was the macho head of the family, and sought to continue the vendetta through her, whereas everyone else saw that she wasn't responsible for ruining Vittorio's planned marriage to Luisa. Maybe they'd be particularly friendly to her, to compensate for his pigheadedness.

'You'll be introduced to everyone and thoroughly questioned, but unless you make a play for the menfolk you'll be accepted,' he said sardonically.

'I'm not in the least bit interested in the men of your family,' said Jemma coolly. 'I find Italian males far too insincere.'

He glared at her over his coffee-cup. 'You have much to learn about my race. Be polite to my family, Jemma. Afternoon tea is an important social occasion, and my mother is hoping it will be a success.'

'I wouldn't do anything to upset your mother,' she said quietly.

That earned her a quizzical look. 'At least you recognise a good woman when you see one,' he said drily. 'If you find that any of my aunts are beginning to interrogate you too intimately, then catch my eye and I'll come and rescue you. The ordeal won't last too long, anyway. I shall tell them you have studying to do, before and after dinner.'

The slave-driving was to continue into the night, it seemed. 'Study? Italian?'

'No, no. We'll speak in English together and here at home until you feel less alien. Later we'll concentrate on improving your speech.'

'I was told I spoke fluently,' she said bridling a little. It was probably the only thing that gained her any marks in her finals!

'True. But you speak without feeling. You see, a sentence can be said in ten different ways and thus have ten different meanings. Italian is a . . . romantic language, a language of the heart.' His mouth had grown so sensual that tiny, sharp daggers were slicing through her body at the thought of its warm pressure. 'You speak with your head. It is like listening to an army sergeant giving orders to a group of recruits. It grates on my ears the way you speak. You need to caress your sentences with emotion. I will teach you how.'

'I bet you will,' she said sarcastically. She needed to keep a verbal distance from him, not sink into the sensually emotive Italian that she had heard him speak!

'Unlike the Mortimer family, the Vasaris are not betting men,' he said silkily.

Jemma whitened. 'That was cruel!' she breathed.

'It was,' he acknowledged. 'But it reminds you why you're here.'

'To labour all day and half the night, it seems,' she said.

'Most Italians work those hours,' he answered. 'At least, the ones who want to succeed, or who have responsibilities. If it will make you less resentful, you might like to know that my hours are even longer.'

'So what will I be studying?' she asked.

'The law. You'll help your clients more successfully if you are fully conversant with Law Forty-Three for instance, which concerns the transfer of funds from abroad. You'll need to know the procedure to be followed during a purchase, the Document of Intent, the *compromesso,* use of surveyors, notaries, advocates, the different registers and agricultural waivers . . .'

'Yes. I get the message,' she said tightly. It sounded far more daunting than she'd imagined. No wonder Brian had shied away from getting invlved.

'It seems worse than it is. You're intelligent and will pick it up soon enough,' he said. 'And I think you are very determined. Yes?' His brow arched in mocking query.

'When do we start?' she asked calmly.

He dabbed his mouth with a scarlet napkin. 'In five minutes.'

A few moments later, when she ran down the steps to join him, she felt an odd nervousness. They were going to spend day after day together, sometimes in isolated countryside. The pressure on both of them would be strong: she found him incredibly attractive and he had a point or two to prove. There was only one thing for it, she thought: The Ice Queen Cometh!

As she slid in, she couldn't help but see the long stretch of his legs in the low-slung car—a Maserati this time, but still in the aggressive red he favoured. He'd slung a white jumper around his shoulders and slipped on a pair of sunglasses. Their fingers met when he took the seat-belt clip from her and fastened it securely, and she was sure that the rise in his chest was from irritation that she'd dared to touch him. Whatever the reason, she found herself wishing he didn't project such a potent masculinity. His personality seemed to fill the car interior and reach out to smother her. It was a pity he was such a splendid example of male supremacy. She deliberately cultivated a look of indifference.

But the landscape threatened to soften her up. The warm sun lit the tumbling houses of Montevecchio with a pure, clear light and, as they descended to the valley, she looked back repeatedly, feeling herself relax. As far as she could, she'd enjoy everything, only putting on the deep freeze if he overstepped the mark.

'Where are we going?' she asked, as they left the side road and roared off on the Via Flamina.

'Spoleto. I thought we'd start with something straightforward. Rambling estates can be difficult to itemise. I won't expect you to do any valuations to start with—that will come much later.'

Jemma's eyes sparkled at the thought that she was at last doing some challenging work. As they sped along, the mountains on one side, the fertile river valley on the other, she sensed the tension leave Vittorio's body, and he shrugged off his jumper, settling down into his seat.

Soon it became very warm, and he gave her several glances, as if making up his mind to ask her something. 'Would you mind if we drove without the car hood?' he suggested eventually.

'I'd love it!'

He pulled into the side and she helped eagerly, jumping into the car when they'd finished with all the excitement of a young girl.

'Hold tight,' he grinned, catching her infectious enthusiasm. After a quick check behind for traffic, he stamped on the accelerator and they shot away, the sensation of rushing air making Jemma lift her face and laugh with pleasure.

'You like speed, Jemma?' he yelled, a wicked gleam in his eyes.

She nodded, and felt her back press into the seat as the car surged forwards. Wisps of hair had worked loose from her severe pleat and were whipping around her face. The slipstream buffeted Vittorio's hair like a

capricious wind in a wheatfield. He was concentrating
intently on the road, his eyes narrowed, his nostrils
flaring in excitement. He, too, was grinning with the
pleasure of freedom that the open road and the open car
were generating in both of them.

Gradually they slowed as signs began to come up for
Spoleto. They exchanged smiles and Jemma's heart
flipped briefly at the transient warmth in Vittorio's
expression. Frantically she smoothed back the stray
wisps.

'I'm not going to look tidy now,' she said with a
nervous laugh.

'You look very elegant, glowing and a little more
human,' he said wryly.

Colour stained Jemma's golden cheeks. She laid her
arm along the warm metal of the door and scanned the
landscape, trying to divert her thoughts from the
potentially dangerous man beside her. She saw that the
wide river valley had narrowed and above the fields of
pumpkins rose Spoleto, set in pine-clad hills.

It was market-day, and the square was filled with
colourful disorder, as donkeys were unloaded and stalls
set up with strange-looking cheeses, red, yellow and
green peppers, huge tomatoes, strings of sausages and
salami, and everything ranging from iron bedsteads to
lingerie. Jemma was entranced as they walked through
the *piazza,* and couldn't resist dawdling. Unaware,
Vittorio strode on alone. Suddenly he was by her side,
catching her elbow and leading her away at a rapid pace.

'I'm sorry, but there's no time to stop,' he said
firmly.

'Don't I get a little time for sightseeing?' she asked
breathlessly, trying to keep up with his long stride.

'No.'

Thanks for nothing, she thought. 'I need to know about Spoleto's attractions for the blurb on the house we're going to see,' she said with sudden inspiration.

'True,' he said, without slowing his pace. 'Get your notebook out. Spoleto, loved by St Francis and admired by Michelangelo . . . you're not taking this down.'

'Oh, really, Vittorio!' she said, stopping in exasperation.

He grinned and placed his hands up in defence. 'All right, all right! We'll sprinkle our sessions on learning how to describe properties with learning how to identify the things tourists enjoy. I'll show you around some time.'

'Today?' she asked, hopefully.

'No. I can't spare the time.'

'I shan't need you,' she said quickly. She was perfectly capable of sightseeing on her own. 'I have an International Driving Certificate. I could borrow one of the family cars.'

'I don't want you driving around on your own, Jemma, until it is well known who you are. Once it's common knowledge that you're under the protection of the Vasaris, then you will be perfectly safe. Till then, someone must always be with you.'

'And that someone must be you, I suppose?' she asked sourly, vowing to talk to his mother about his extraordinary denial of her freedom.

'I'm your protector. Of course it will be me. I'm certainly not letting you loose with my defenceless brothers, even if they do have plenty of free time. This is the house, let's get to work,' he said sharply.

The old village house had a ramp which led down to

stables and a *cantina* cut out of the rock. The brick-floored kitchen, beamed like the rest of the house, opened on to a small *piazza,* and at the rear was a small garden with an olive grove. Jemma scribbled away, writing notes as Vittorio guided her in what she should look for, conscious all the time of his gently murmuring voice and all-too-near presence.

'Oh, there's a balcony!' she cried, stepping on to a tiny, rickety platform.

'Careful,' he warned, from inside the room. 'It needs repairing.'

Tentatively Jemma tried her weight on the smooth boards till she reached the carved wooden balustrade. It looked down into the narrow street not far below, and across to a similar house with a little balcony. Into her mind came words from *Romeo and Juliet,* and she sighed a romantic sigh, wishing her lover was there, courting her with eloquent phrases.

'Please come in, the struts aren't safe,' called Vittorio.

Dreamily she turned around to see him hovering tensely, his handsome face catching the bright sun so that he looked like an Apollo.

Just then, there was a crack and Jemma found herself falling. She grabbed at something and found it was Vittorio's arm. Her nails dragged down it as she slipped, then his hand clamped around her wrist firmly.

'Hold on, there's no real danger. I'll pull you up,' he called.

Hold on! What else did he think she'd do? Jemma looked cautiously around. Most of the balcony was hanging drunkenly from the side of the house, but she wasn't far from the ground. Vittorio was clinging to the

door-jamb, one leg hooked around it, an arm outstretched. Slowly he hauled her up, and she tried to
relieve him of some of her weight by hanging on to any
bit of the balcony that looked stable.

His big hands wrapped around her body, drawing her
to him, and she laid her head briefly against his chest.
All the time, she'd been unafraid. With Vittorio there,
holding her, she knew she was safe and that it was only a
matter of time before she was in his arms.

'That was pretty silly,' he said in her ear.

'I was being Juliet,' she said as if that explained
everything.

Vittorio eased her away so that he could search her
face. 'And who am I?' he said in liquid tones.

Jemma widened her blue eyes. 'The Nurse, of course.
She's the protector.'

His roar of laughter startled her. 'Well, keeping in
role, I order you to brush yourself down, fix your hair
and I'll clean up that graze on your arm.'

She grinned back, obeying him. 'Thanks. I know it
wasn't far to fall, but I would have ended up bloodied
and bruised. You have quick reflexes. It was a silly thing
to do and I should have listened to you. But . . .'

'I know. You were looking for Romeo,' he said drily.
'Try Verona next time.'

The incident seemed to have eased the relationship.
While he dabbed at the graze with his white handkerchief, dipped in icy water from the well, he delivered a
silly, soothing patter as if he was her fussy Nurse.
Jemma kept giggling and he kept scolding her incessant
fidgeting.

'Right,' he said, when he had finished to his satisfaction. 'Make a note about the balcony. Next, describe the

view.'

'I haven't finished the last item yet,' she said, with a frown at the way he had come to stand close behind her.

'Where are you up to?' His head dipped, bringing his face near to hers, and she only had to lean her cheek a little to the left to feel the warm smoothness of his skin. Or he might turn, and his lips would be able to reach her jaw. Jemma clenched her teeth so that her head stayed rigidly in place and she did neither of these things, assailed by the achingly familiar fragrance of his body. Her hand faltered.

'Must you stand so close?' she snapped, as his warm breath fanned her cheek.

'Bothers you, does it?' he asked with a lazy smile.

'I detest inhaling garlic.' That his breath was sweet and utterly disruptive to her senses was a fact she didn't intend to communicate!

'Garlic!' he roared, catching her waist again and spinning her around. 'You tell me . . .' There was a sudden change in his face and he laughed softly, still spanning her waist with his strong fingers. 'You dare to tease me?' he grinned.

'Someone has to,' she said crisply. 'You take yourself far too seriously.'

'Hmmm. That's true. It's a long time since I relaxed. So you think I should unbend a little?'

'Definitely. You're very formal for a man of your age.'

'A man . . .!' His eyes danced with laughter. 'Now I remember why I used to enjoy arguing with you. I'd found someone who wasn't afraid to use every trick in the book to topple me from whatever stance I was taking. So, you think I'm a bit formal? Perhaps stuffy?'

'It's understandable,' she said in a kindly tone, glad to divert him from his unknowingly sensual assault. 'A man in your position tends to get set in his ways.'

'Straight between the eyes as usual,' he muttered. 'All right, I'll do my best. We've done the trapeze act and the Strong Man act, and this day seems to be turning into a circus anyway. We might as well bow to Fate and go along with the madness. Shall we have a little fun every now and then?'

If he'd said that during breakfast, she would have suspected his motives and wondered what his idea of fun might be. As it was, his face was utterly open and stripped of its cynicism. Jemma was tired of fighting, tired of being alternately miserable and on her guard. She flashed him a beaming smile.

'Fun,' she agreed.

'At least we both know who's playing the part of the clown,' he said.

With a broad grin, he released his hold on her waist and she placed her trusting hand in his for the walk back to the car.

'I'm hungry,' he said, stopping at a stall. 'How about some *crostini?*'

She looked into his smiling eyes. 'Love some,' she said. 'Three, if that's all right.'

'*Three?*'

'I didn't have much breakfast,' she said with pretended dignity. 'You kept growling at me and it spoiled my appetite.'

Vittorio was already juggling with the rounds of hot toasted bread and cheese, each one wrapped in a fold of paper. 'Perhaps I ought to growl at you again,' he laughed, indicating with his full hands that she would have to get the money from his wallet.

Jemma slipped it from his back trouser-pocket, paid the stallholder and tried to push the loose change into his side pocket without coming into too much contact with his warm body. She took her share of *crostini* from him and they wandered through the town in the sunshine, biting into the crusty bread and enjoying the sharp, rough cheese.

'Is the breadcrumb and cheese moustache *de rigueur* nowadays?' enquired Vittorio with interest.

'It's an ancient method of storing food for later in a readily available place,' she giggled, discovering with the tip of her finger that he was exaggerating. There were only a few crumbs and a slick of cheese.

'Wish I'd thought of that,' he said earnestly. 'Is the store only for you, or can I raid it?'

She drew back warily. 'You smother your own face with cheese,' she said quickly, beginning to lick off the unladylike remnants of her snack.

He chuckled and held open the car door for her. 'Spoilsport.'

'Where to now?' she asked.

'Bandit country,' he answered. 'Wild boar, wolves.'

She gave a girly scream and wrung her hands, then patted him comfortingly on the shoulder. 'Don't be afraid, Nursy. I'll flick dollops of *crostini* at them. I saved one or two bits for just such an emergency.'

'It sounds as if you know how to deal with bandits and wolves,' he observed drily.

'Oh, yes. You just show them you've got more guts,' she said airily, choosing not to acknowledge his meaning.

'Not literally, I hope,' he murmured.

She laughed and let out a contented sigh as he swung the Maserati on to a narrow country road and they began to climb into the high mountains. Sure enough, he hadn't been joking—there were signs warning that the land had been reserved for wild-boar hunting.

'I must apologise for the lack of wolves and bandits,' he said amiably. 'Must be their day off.'

'*Are* there wolves?' she asked uncertainly.

'Oh, yes, honestly. Don't ever go into the woods or hills on your own. And,' he added, reversing in order to negotiate a sharp hairpin bend, 'don't chance topping your gold locks with a red riding hood.'

'I won't,' she promised. 'It would be like waving a red rag to a bull, wouldn't it?'

He shook his head in despair at her confusing simile and they were still laughing when he drove up to a tiny cottage, nestling in the woods.

'Belonged to the Three Bears,' he said, straight-faced. 'Go and check out the porridge.' He pushed back his seat and relaxed, placing his hands smugly on his stomach.

'On my own?' she asked, seeing he had no intention of stirring.

'I want to see how you get on without any prompting. I'll stay out here and toot the horn if I see any wolves.'

'Then what happens?' Jemma asked uncertainly.

'I drive off to a safe place and watch the *crostini* fly,' he grinned.

Amused, Jemma picked up her notebook and took the key from his hand. As she systematically took details of the little house, she had to keep pushing down the urge to think about Vittorio and how easily they'd fallen into a bantering camaraderie. It was a side of him she hadn't seen before, and she wasn't sure she wanted to *like* him. The day had turned out quite differently from the way she had imagined. Instead of his implacable hatred and her cold silences there was laughter and teasing. And, she thought soberly, you only teased people you were fond of. Well, she was enjoying it all too much to go back to being frosty. Let the future take care of itself, she decided recklessly; the present was *fun*.

She snapped the book shut and demurely returned to present it to Vittorio, standing beside the car like a well-behaved schoolgirl.

'Do I get ten out of ten, sir?' she asked, her lashes lowered.

'You get the school prize,' he said laconically.

She looked at him dubiously. 'What's that?'

'Me.'

She was about to back away when he began to shake his head in reproof. 'I'm sorry to disappoint you, but you haven't earned the prize after all. You've omitted something.'

Her face fell in dismay. She'd tried hard to remember everything.

'Electricity,' he said.

'There wasn't any!'

'Exactly.' He smiled, his eyes crinkling. 'So, what . . .'

There was a rustling in the undergrowth behind Jemma, as if a heavy animal was prowling around. His damn wolf! Her head whipped around just in time to see a pair of brightly gleaming eyes. Without thinking twice, she flung herself into the car on top of Vittorio, who caught her with a surprised grunt, quickly feeding her body down on to his lap and blinking at her in astonishment. She clung to him fiercely, her eyes huge.

Instead of driving away to safety, he remained motionless, just holding her, and she became aware of another danger as his powerful body tuned in to hers. Jemma's skin began to prickle at the electrical charges that escaped from every one of his pores, despite the fact that he still wasn't doing anything; just holding her, watching her, his mouth cresting in that damnable soft sensuality, his eyes liquid blue and bold.

'The wolf——' she croaked.

'Is here,' he grunted, and brought his mouth down hard on hers.

CHAPTER SIX

THERE seemed to be an explosion of energy between them: the wild beasts in the undergrowth were nothing to the wild beasts within their own bodies. Vittorio's mouth drove into Jemma's so fiercely that she ended up lying across the passenger seat, opening her arms to him and drawing him to her, wanting their bodies to merge. His control had snapped and, with it, hers.

His ardour was far too advanced to allow for preliminaries; if he had held back, she would have made her own demands. In response to her urgent whimpering in the back of her throat, his lips ruthlessly forced her mouth open and immediately she felt the hot thrust of his sweet tongue that flickered so erotically that the sensation had her clutching at him wildly from the insatiable hunger it aroused. The years of restraint and repression of her longing to be loved by Vittorio were in danger of being swept away by his urgent assault. More than anything she wanted to explore his mouth too, shut out the reasons for them to stay apart, and *know* him.

Tentatively, her tongue curled forwards, touched his, tasted the sweetness, and he erupted into a growling fury, invading her mouth more deeply and thoroughly, plundering her with his hands, till she realised that he had undone the back of her dress and was beginning to slip it from her shoulders.

Too far, too soon, hammered Jemma's brain as his teeth savaged her throat.

'No, Vittorio! I don't want . . .'

'You do! *Gesù Maria!* We are both starving! Don't tease me now, Jemma.'

'*No!*' She rapped out, squeezing her legs together as his fingers crawled inexorably up her long, golden thigh.

To her unutterable relief, he paused, raised his marauding lips and met her hostile eyes.

'Beautiful Jemma, you want me,' he said huskily. 'Let me lift you from the car and we'll make love amid the poppies. Let me love you, Jemma,' his mouth whispered in her ear, travelling around its small pink shell, sending Jemma crazy.

'No, I won't. I only turned to you from fear. Oh, my God! The wolf!' she cried, trying to sit up and pushing his hands away.

'There's no danger,' he said, amused. 'Not out there, anyway.' He helped her up with a deep sigh and sat watching while she pulled her dress—and herself— together. 'That was a donkey you saw.'

Jemma glared. 'You might have told me!'

He shrugged. 'And miss all the fun? Besides, you didn't give me a chance. One minute we were talking about electricity, the next we were producing it.'

So he'd felt it, too! Jemma blushed and lifted her head proudly. 'No more playing around,' she said, sounding sharp.

'Who was playing? You're difficult to please. Lunch, then?' he murmured. 'Siena?'

'Lunch,' she agreed. 'Siena.'

She was well aware that he wasn't annoyed or frustrated at all; in fact he appeared to be rather pleased with himself. No doubt he imagined that she'd be ready to jump into his arms any time he beckoned, now he'd got to first base. So she answered his cheerful remarks with icy silences and he soon got the message, refraining from taunting her sexually. It didn't dampen his spirits much, though. On the contrary, it increased his amusement.

He guided her through the dark, tall houses of Siena to the *campo* and, try as she might, Jemma couldn't prevent herself from uttering a small gasp of pleasure at the beautiful shell-shaped *piazza,* enclosed by towering golden buildings. They ordered spaghetti at the Bar Mangia, which faced a slender rose-red tower, rising three hundred feet above a castellated *palazzo*. Jemma fed the pigeons some of her roll, while Vittorio watched her with lazy eyes that made her squirm inwardly.

'I'm sorry,' he said quietly, spreading his hands in a Latin gesture. 'When you landed in my arms, I just couldn't help myself. It seemed too good an opportunity to lose. Whether I like it or not, you do tend to increase my pulse rate on occasions.'

She lifted wary eyes. 'Is that how you normally carry on with women?' she asked sharply.

'No. Only the ones who jump on to my lap.'

'You know perfectly . . .' She gave a brief laugh. 'It must have seemed I was throwing myself at you,' she admitted.

'I'd forgotten the real reason,' he said casually.

Jemma's stomach churned. 'Real . . . reason?' she repeated in an unnaturally high voice.

'Part of your circus performance.'

Jemma felt grateful to him for lightening the situation. 'It took years to perfect,' she said airily.

'I can't wait to see your finale,' he murmured.

'Don't hold your breath,' she shot back, reassured by

his amusement. 'So . . . am I to understand that there'll be no more wolves?'

He nodded solemnly, but Jemma could still see the desire lurking in his eyes, telling her that she only had to murmur a suggestion and she could be in his arms again, tasting him, feeling the hardness of his body that promised a release for her, locked in passion. She tore her gaze away to stare sightlessly across the *campo*. From the far side came a whoop of joy and she focused on a sturdy little boy aged about six, who detached himself from his parents and ran across the *campo,* flapping his hands merrily at the pigeons. She smiled to see his innocent happiness, but her smile turned to concern as he stumbled and fell heavily. Before she could even rise from her chair, Vittorio had leapt up, his long legs taking him to the child before anyone else. He gathered the yelling boy into his arms and carried him back to the café.

An imperious lift of his finger brought a waiter scurrying up and Vittorio ordered warm, disinfected water, cloths and a towel.

The man hurried away and Vittorio switched back to English, for the boy was complaining loudly in that language.

'Ah, such a bad wound,' murmured Vittorio. 'Let me see now, you must be the thousandth brave man to be injured in this place.'

'Wow!' The boy stopped wailing to listen.

'Uh-huh, all tough, handsome men, who fought for their lives and for the city of Siena, driving back wicked bandits and invaders. Strong men, like you and me.'

'Wow!'

Jemma tried not to giggle. The boy's parents arrived,

but the child wasn't interested. All he wanted was for Vittorio to bathe his wounds and tell him about brave men.

With the waiter reverently holding a bowl, Vittorio gravely cleaned the badly grazed knees and gently removed particles of grit from the little boy's palms.

'This Nursy business is becoming a habit,' he muttered in an aside to Jemma.

'Not too good for your macho image,' she whispered, thinking idly that Vittorio would still be all male with an apron around his waist.

He chuckled and turned his attention back to the wide-eyed boy. 'It's exciting to think,' said Vittorio in his warm, rich voice, 'that probably hundreds of years ago a young man fell in the same spot, struggling to his knees, weak, sword still in his hand and too brave to give up . . .' He gestured for a towel and gently wiped the wounds dry. '. . . so he fought on with the Sienese people till the enemy had been turned out of the city and at last they could close the great gates with a satisfying clang . . .'

'Clang!' crowed the boy, delighted.

Vittorio grinned at the child and Jemma felt a heart-wrenching tug. The tenderness and sweetness in Vittorio's face was making him too human, too kind. It was difficult discovering that he could be gentle and humorous beneath that haughty attitude. She wanted to keep hating him, she wanted her image of him to be of a man steeped in evil, and here he was, getting a little boy's grimy hands all over his pale blue trousers and blood on his snow-white shirt. He wasn't acting fairly, she thought resentfully. He ought to snarl and leer and yell. *That* she could deal with.

'There. You are mended. Forgive me, *signor, signora,*' said Vittorio, rising with a small bow, 'but I thought that your precious son ought not to take the pigeon droppings of Siena home in his bloodstream.'

'Oh! No, of course not, thank you, thank you . . .'

Overwhelmed by his charm, they nodded and smiled their thanks, dragging the protesting child away, scolding him for running off.

'You're looking very pensive, Jemma,' murmured Vittorio softly.

She sighed. 'I was thinking it might be nice to change places with that little boy.'

'That's a little drastic. If you want to sit on my knee and hear stories, then that can be arranged without going that far.'

'That isn't why I'd want to be him!' she said in exasperation.

'Tell me why,' he crooned, stroking her hand to placate her.

She snatched it away. 'So that I could be young and innocent and not constantly ogled.'

'Ah. Cue for more work, I think.'

'What happened to our siesta?' she protested.

'If you want me to find a quiet spot and lay down a rug for us . . .'

'No!' she said firmly. Her will-power wasn't very strong today. She didn't want to risk waking in his arms. If he ever allowed her to sleep in the first place, she thought gloomily.

'*Allora.* Two more properties and then home for tea.'

It was hard on her nerves, incredibly hard. He was so *nice.* If only he'd be vindictive, like in the old days, she thought with irrational longing! She felt quite guilty for enjoying her work so much.

Their return journey was full of laughter and teasing about ferocious donkeys. Jemma was tired and happy when they parted to freshen up for tea, and she hurried through her shower, humming quietly to herself. Maybe they could both put the past behind them and take each day as it came. At some stage she'd explain about Dave and persuade Vittorio to admit that his attitude towards Luisa had been harsh. But then where would that leave her? Still in love with a man who carried a torch for her dead sister-in-law, and who was destined to marry into the Italian aristocracy. Careful, she told herself. Keep a sensible distance.

As she slipped into a lime-green shot silk suit, and clasped a navy kid belt around her narrow waist, she drummed it into herself that Vittorio might want to bed her, but he was, after all, hunting for richer game.

And that was borne out during tea. It was a very grandly casual affair: dozens of women of all ages dressed to the nines, a handful of suave men, and what seemed like hordes of dark-eyed children. The latter launched themselves on Vittorio in boisterous greeting and it was a long time before he surfaced from tumbling with them on the floor. Jemma was greeted with more decorum, and as the tea trolley rolled in laden with cakes and pastries and every kind of tea she could imagine—and, she noticed with astonishment, whisky for the men—the senior female relatives began to quiz her.

Vittorio, she noticed, had been bagged by a bevy of beautiful female cousins. When she remarked jokingly on this, one of the aunts smiled fondly at Vittorio and patted her knee.

'He is wise to surround himself with women, so the one he loves is unknown. Only when he is very, very sure, he told me once, will he propose marriage. A woman will need to be very special, to marry *Il Conte*. It is not an easy job to run an estate like this *and* to satisfy a man as passionate as Vittorio.'

'And how *you* know he's passionate?' glared the Marchesa, her stern face breaking into a wicked grin at the horror on her sister's face. 'Didi's right,' she said to the smiling Jemma. 'I feel almost sorry for the Vasari men. They always seem to pick women who are downright difficult. I gave his father such agonies during our courtship! I do hope you argue with Vittorio a lot.'

'Oh—er—yes, we do rather.'

'I thought so,' said the Marchesa with satisfaction. 'Ah, those magnificent hours of making up!' Jemma shot her a suspicious glance. Sometimes she didn't know what to make of the Marchesa. 'Look at his cousin Carla,' she continued blithely, 'dreaming into his eyes. He'd soon get tired of that.'

'Would he?' murmured Jemma uncertainly. His gaze lingered on raven-headed Carla's tiny face as if it might be rather a long time before he was tired of her.

'I think you're wrong,' said Didi. 'Carla's perfect for him. Can't you see?'

Jemma saw. And felt. Ashamed of the awful, jabbing jealousy, she forced herself to be polite to the ladies and was relieved when Vittorio was claimed by the children again. Ignoring his immaculately cut charcoal-and-white-striped suit, he led them in a mad chase around the garden, ending by capturing as many of them as he could in his strong arms and carrying their wriggling bodies back to their mothers. Jemma envied the affection he received from all his family as they took their leave. From the elderly to the young, he was kissed and hugged with vigour, his eyes gentle, his face joyous and churning up Jemma's insides so much that she had to turn away.

Engulfed in a reluctant tenderness towards him, she settled down to her studies, realising at dinner that she had no idea what she'd learnt. The meal was noisy, with everyone discussing family gossip at the same time, and she looked from one to the other—happy, beautiful people, genuinely interested and caring about their relatives. Her studies after dinner were as fruitless as her work before. All she could think of was Vittorio's Jekyll-and-Hyde character: how much she liked him until he became angry, and how cruel he could be then.

Yet one thing puzzled her. However hurt he'd been by Luisa's rejection, she couldn't imagine him disowning her. Family meant too much to the Vasaris and, even if he'd contemplated such a thing for a moment, it didn't seem likely that the others would accept his ban.

There was something they were withholding from her, and she'd find out what it was. Not from Vittorio, because it pained him to talk about his cousin, but from Rico. He'd tell her everything. She'd manoeuvre a time when they could be alone and clear up the mystery that nagged at her so irritatingly.

However, for the next few days, she had no time to herself and certainly no opportunity to speak privately to Rico.

With consummate charm and effortless ease, Vittorio managed not only to teach her a great deal about the Italian properties they visited together, but to scatter happiness indiscriminately around him. Wherever they went, whoever they met, from wealthy lawyers to peasant farmers, the conversation was always conducted with warmth and friendship. He evidently loved his country and its people, loved to be out in the 'Green Heart of Italy'. Jemma was with him from dawn to dusk, and never once did she catch a glimpse of the vicious, spiteful part of his nature. He seemed too good to be true, but whether she wanted it to happen or not, he was reclaiming her senses and she had once again fallen for him.

As he had once promised, he took her to the family church in Montevecchio, and there in the cool, restful serenity of the soaring Gothic pillars they sat and admired the startling cobalt-blue stained glass in the huge rose window above the altar.

'You see, I was right,' smiled Vittorio, looking from her eyes to her dress—since he'd insisted she chose a blue to match her eyes.

'It's a different dress,' she said, trying not to let the warm weakness invade any further.

'I know. I remember the last one.'

'You do?'

'Of course. I remember every single word, every single gesture. I shall be married here one day,' he said, abruptly changing the subject.

A spasm of pain crossed her face. 'You have someone in mind?' she asked faintly.

'No. My aunts and other relations keep hauling suitable girls in front of me and I drink tea with them, compliment them on their hair or their dresses or the shape of their noses and think how docile they all are,' he said gloomily.

'That's because you're used to your mother,' she

said, a little happier that he was still unclaimed. 'She's very unorthodox. Your Aunt Didi nearly had a fit when the Marchesa accused her of having an affair with you.'

He grinned. 'I think my mother could best be described as wayward. That's what my father called her once, in the middle of a terrible argument that raged up and down the *palazzo*. "You're a wayward hussy," he yelled from the top of the grand staircase. "And aren't you glad!" my mother yelled back. They both started to laugh and ran to each other, meeting in a tangle of arms and legs and laughter in the middle of the stairs, and I discreetly got my brothers out of the way.'

Jemma was laughing. 'She's wonderful,' she said with affection.

'I know.' His face grew thoughtful. 'How I find a woman remotely as satisfying as she is I don't know.'

Pain arced through Jemma's body. They were both silent and after a few minutes, the strangely sad Vittorio raised his eyebrow at her in unspoken query. She nodded and they left the church to begin work.

That day they lunched by the shores of Lake Trasimeno, and their rather quiet, reserved attitude towards one another was relaxed by the laughter of children enjoying a Punch and Judy show. When she teasingly suggested that the Italians had copied a famous English beach occupation, he surprised her by saying that Pulcinella was playing to the crowds in Naples in the seventeenth century. After that, they began to swap favourite childhood pastimes and Jemma floundered secretly as she sank deeper and deeper into his web. It was a pointless journey, she told herself. But one she seemed incapable of escaping.

Today, as on all days, she was dreading the siesta.

He usually drove to a lovely spot, sheltered from the road, and they rested, sometimes talking lazily, reading the paper, or dozing after the heavy lunch.

Before they'd left that morning he'd suggested she might care to bring a swimsuit, and she'd deliberately left it behind. The whole business of dressing and undressing and drying would be far too provocative!

Vittorio led the way from the car along a narrow path through a dark wood to a small lake of almost bottle-green water.

'Magical, isn't it?' he murmured, as she spread out the rug.

'Move that branch,' she answered.

With a smile, he did so and flung himself down, staring up at the canopy of poplars and willow trees, whose leaves made a delicate tracery against the deep blue sky. Jemma sat down cautiously, hugging her knees and gazing into the dark, mysterious water. Its surface was satin-smooth, reflecting the bowing willow trees, and she almost wished she'd brought her costume. Then she thought of the sensual experience of that silken water caressing her body and the intimacy of swimming there with Vittorio, and decided she'd made a wise choice after all.

Vittorio sat up close to her. 'How long can this last, Jemma?' he asked softly.

'About an hour,' she said briskly, choosing to misunderstand him.

'You're a terrible woman. I mean the friendship between us,' he chided gently.

'Will it end?' Her voice shook at the thought.

'*Amore!*' he murmured, his long, well shaped hand reaching around to take her hand.

'That will end it,' she whispered, pulling away.

He grunted, lay back again and closed his eyes. Jemma's heart ached with longing, She looked down at him in despair, misery written all over her face. She wanted him to love her, not to feel a mixture of desire and contempt. Maybe, she mused, yearning to be held tenderly, that was all he had left, now that his capacity for love had disappeared with Luisa.

Drowsily his eyes flickered and he held out his hand in friendly invitation.

'Lie down, Jemma. Rest. I'm not going to attack you. I feel sleepy. I worked till nearly two-thirty this morning. I can't rest while you're so tense. Please? You could tell me a bedtime story,' he said hopefully.

She smiled, extended her arm and their fingers touched and clasped. She let him pull her down, accepting the friendly overture and curling up beside him in the protective circle of his arm. If he tries to touch me now, if he breaks the mood, I'll never forgive him! she said to herself apprehensively.

Vittorio gave her shoulder a slight squeeze and tucked her comfortably into his side. She allowed her hand to rest on his gently rising chest and his big palm covered it warmly. He gave a contented sigh and was still.

With the leaves whispering secrets overhead and the occasional drone of a bee in the background, her tensed muscles relaxed, one by one. She must have slept a little, because she came around to find Vittorio bending over her, smiling, and brushing wisps of hair from her face. The air became suddenly thick and the world stopped moving, as if holding its breath. A kiss, light as a butterfly wing, brushed her lips.

'I'm going for a swim,' he muttered, and disappeared

from her view.

The world spun once more. Jemma sat up and unashamedly watched him strip to bathing trunks, the beautiful golden body hard and muscled as he moved, and in a flash of honey skin he had run to the edge of the lake and dived in, sending black ripples towards her. She held the vision of his powerful frame in her mind as his head reappeared and he began to swim.

'Come on in!' he shouted. 'It's like swimming in the Arctic!'

'Not on your life!' she called, standing up to see him more clearly. 'I might meet a penguin.'

'Wrong bit of the globe. You're neurotic about wild animals, aren't you?'

Grinning, she bent down and aimed a small branch near him. He swam to it, grabbed it with his teeth and started for the bank. He moved so beautifully in the water, cleaving it cleanly, his bright yellow hair like a clump of wheat in a meadow. Then he was hauling himself out, water cascading from his body, and Jemma had to avert her eyes at the sheer physical ache that it had aroused in the pit of her stomach.

He threw away the stick, dark intent in his eyes as he slicked back his dripping hair. 'I'm coming to make you swim,' he threatened.

'You can't,' she said quickly. 'I didn't bring my costume.'

A slow smile spread over his face. 'Why?'

'I didn't want to.'

'Liar.'

'What!'

'You were afraid,' he breathed, advancing. 'Just like me.'

'I don't know what you mean,' she croaked, her heart hammering violently in her ribs.

A few feet away he paused,'I'm afraid that when we make love our friendship will end, and it's something I value,' he said simply.

'When? *When* we make love?' she cried incredulously. 'You're taking a lot for granted!'

'We like each other, we desire each other. I can't think of any reason why we shouldn't. I'm not exactly unaware of the chemistry between us, Jemma,' he said, pulling her down to the grass and holding her with his eyes.

'I can think of plenty,' she said coldly. 'One of them being my morality.'

'I'm sorry,' he said, imprisoning her by her shoulders, 'but you can't plead innocence.'

Jemma felt her insides twist. 'What you saw . . .'

'Will remain in my memory for ever. I saw a woman panting with desire, her hair cascading over her bare shoulders. I saw two unbelievably luscious, creamy breasts, tumbling into a rough thug's giant paw. And I near killed you both,' he breathed. 'But don't try to tell me you were rolling on the bed in an innocent boy and girl game, Jemma, because I just couldn't believe it.'

'When your pride is hurt, it really takes a knock, doesn't it?' she snapped.

'Don't be like that,' he crooned. 'It was so good, earlier on, when we kissed . . .'

'Vittorio, you're expert at lowering a woman's resistance, as I'm sure you know. But I'd better save you a lot of effort and say that I'm not as easy as you seem to think.'

'That's true!' he said with feeling.

'I like you. And I don't want the friendship spoilt. Whatever was between us in the past *is* past. I've made a vow, Vittorio, one I'm going to keep. Only the man I choose to love and marry will be my lover.'

'Marriage?' His eyebrow quirked. 'You put a high price on something that has already been lost. I hope you find what you want, Jemma.'

'Thank you,' she said briskly. She'd leave him in ignorance of her virginity and save herself heartache. 'We've cleared the air. We both know where we stand.'

Vittorio was biting his lip. 'And you're after marriage?' he queried, his face hard.

'I didn't say that.'

'Don't entertain any ideas of changing your sights from me to my brothers, will you?' he murmured in a menacing tone. 'Because if you try anything like that, I'll teach you a lesson.'

'Rico would make a charming husband,' she snapped, 'if it wasn't for the fact that I'd have you as a brother-in-law!'

'*Basta!*'

Vittorio jumped up, towelled himself vigorously and dressed in a temper. The rest of the afternoon they hardly addressed a word to each other, and Jemma found how easily joy could turn to emptiness.

That evening, she decided her shattered defences needed shoring up. For her, clothes had become part of the layer of protection. Dressing smartly made her feel cool and remote—the kind of feelings she generally preferred to exhibit. But after Vittorio's frank explanation of the way he saw her, as a woman who might as well share herself around, she needed a little unqualified admiration for a change.

She'd choose a dress that would appeal to Rico, and to hell with the Count! Tonight, at least, she'd be appreciated by someone. The dress was a long hip-and thigh-hugging black sheath, which moulded to her body and curved over her breasts in tiny pleated fans. It was strapless, and her lovely golden shoulders rose in shocking nakedness above the stark black. In her small earlobes, blue sapphire ear-rings echoed the cold glitter of her eyes.

Her reflection met with her satisfaction. She would salvage some pride. She might have the urge to crawl on the ground to earn Vittorio's regard, but he'd never know. She paused at the top of the broad, sweeping staircase, mentally preparing herself.

'Holy Mary!' breathed Enrico behind her.

His eyes told her everything she wanted to know. 'You like my dress?' she asked with a smile.

'Like!' he croaked, mesmerised by the gentle rise and fall of her breasts. 'You look . . .' He gave a gently savage growl, and Jemma laughed. 'No wonder Vivi's been keeping you so much to himself! He hasn't been so possessive since he was entrusted with . . . Oh! I am not to talk of this.'

'You meant Luisa?' asked Jemma impulsively. 'Rico, I want to hear. No one will talk to me about her. Can we meet after dinner? Perhaps a walk in the garden?'

His eyes lit up. 'Delighted! But he'll kill me if he knows I've discussed her. After dinner, then. *Permesso?*'

She took his arm, satisfied. Tonight she'd know how much Vittorio loved Luisa.

The entered the dining-room together and immediately she became aware of Vittorio's barely leashed rage at the way Rico was gazing down on her. It made her feel stronger, more in charge of the situation to know that she could get under his skin. All through dinner she flirted gently with Rico, and a devil had got into the Marchesa, who appeared to be encouraging her wicked teasing. Across the table, Vittorio seethed impotently, stirred up by the Marchesa's innocent-sounding remarks. It seemed that Jemma was being given full permission to develop her relationship with Rico.

Afterwards, they all nibbled cherries dipped in brandy, and Gianluca made them laugh with his raucous pub-style playing of the grand piano. Vittorio's brothers chose not to work—and of course he didn't need to, either—and had perfected the art of leisurely entertainment.

Vittorio was bullied to play with Gianluca, who left to pour more drinks, and Vittorio launched absently into 'Liebestraum', with heart-stopping sensitivity. When he finished, there was a silence, and Jemma saw that he didn't even realise anyone was in the room with him.

The Marchesa leaned over and whispered to Jemma. 'Vivi has such a loving touch, is it not so?' she asked wickedly.

'I wouldn't know,' Jemma muttered, angry at her sentimentality,

'Be gentle with him,' said the Marchesa. 'The last years have not been easy.'

'No, I suppose it was hard, not seeing the woman he loved,' said Jemma, thinking how he must have missed Luisa.

'Ah! You know! This is good. We must give him a push, then.'

Jemma hardly heard. She was watching Vittorio's long fingers stroking the keys as if he was caressing a woman. 'I feel a little warm. Perhaps you'd all excuse me if I strolled in the garden.'

'I had hoped you would play something with Vivi,' sighed the Marchesa.

Vittorio stared darkly at Jemma.

'I don't think I'm going to play with him,' she said loudly, with great emphasis. 'Our styles are too different. We don't know the same tunes and I find it hard to harmonise with some people. Besides, I think Vittorio would overpower me and want to take the lead. Enrico, on the other hand . . .' She flashed Rico a brilliant smile. 'Would you escort me?'

'With pleasure,' he said, jumping up.

'No!' Vittorio rose angrily and glared at his brother. 'Rico, it is not proper for you . . .'

'Vivi, you're in the Dark Ages,' Rico laughed. 'If it is perfectly proper for you to sleep all night in a car with Jemma, and to spend days alone with her, then I can take her for a walk in our garden. Surely you don't doubt my honour? If so, I must protest at the insult.'

'I don't doubt your honour.'

Was it her imagination, or was there a nasty crack about *her* honour in that remark? Jemma nodded politely to the Marchesa and reached for Rico's arm, acutely aware of Vittorio's thunderous face.

'*Madonna!* Vivi's so jealous!' laughed Rico as they meandered through the box garden.

More likely he was being protective of his younger brother, thought Jemma. 'Was he like that with Luisa?' she asked idly.

'Oh, yes, the same. You see, Vivi promised to guard

her and keep her safe at her papa's death bed. She was young then, and Vittorio knew where his duty lay.'

'She didn't want to marry him,' said Jemma quickly.

'No, no, he was too stern and protective for her taste. He took his responsibilities seriously.'

Jemma couldn't bear men who ran two sexual codes side by side, shielding the women in their family and indulging freely in sex themselves. 'What I don't understand is, if he cared so much, then how *could* he exile her? How could he forbid her to see the family again?'

'I don't understand,' said Rico, inviting her to sit on a stone seat and laying a handkerchief there first. 'That was Luisa's decision, not Vivi's.'

'Rico, Vittorio stopped Luisa from . . .'

'No, Jemma,' he said firmly. 'He would never do that. I thought you knew the story. My God! When Vittorio had her call, he exploded with rage. Four of us had to drag him from his car—he was going to drive to the airport, fly to London and yell at Luisa till she obeyed him. As for Brian . . .' He shrugged expressively.

Jemma's mouth opened and shut silently. Vittorio must have made up that lie and acted out the drama to cover up his spiteful vendetta.

'I see you don't believe me. But ask anyone here. He loved Luisa. Anyway, when he came back from her funeral he brought some letters she'd kept that he sent, begging her to reconsider her decision. I can show you them if you like.'

'Are you saying that Luisa called Vittorio and said she didn't want to see any of you again?' It seemed incredible.

'After her honeymoon,' said Rico sadly. 'You see, Vittorio had warned her about your brother, he'd tried to dissuade her, but she wanted to enjoy herself. She was so ashamed to discover that Vivi's warnings were justified and couldn't bear him to witness her shame. His anger would have been so great at her dishonour that there would have been bloodshed!'

A numb feeling spread down Jemma's spine. 'What dishonour?' First the gambling, the debts . . . now what?

'Brian gambled,' said Rico, shifting awkwardly.

'And because of that——'

'N-n-no,' he hesitated.

'You must tell me.'

'Vittorio said you were never to know.'

'To hell with him! I have a right to know about my own brother and to understand this stupid feud between our families!' she cried passionately.

'Gently, gently, beautiful Jemma,' he said, holding her trembling hands against his chest. 'You're right. I will tell you. You will not like it. Even on honeymoon, your brother gambled half the night away. And the other half . . . well, it seems the women of Martinique were as willing to share his body as the ones in Surrey.'

'You mean . . . he was *unfaithful?*'

'Frequently. When he was in London with Vittorio, for instance, Brian was always disappearing with women he'd picked up. We wouldn't have known, except we demanded to know the full facts behind Luisa's self-imposed exile.'

'Oh, no,' she moaned weakly.

'You must know how weak Brian was: you were his sister. I know your moral code is different from ours, but for us, well, we were shocked. And Vivi was impossible to contain when he knew of her humiliation.'

'Brian loved her——'

'I think he did, but he couldn't resist other women. Luisa broke her heart, for she has the Vasari pride. No one was to see her shame, and in the end Vivi had to respect her wishes, knowing that a scene with Brian would pain her even more.'

Jemma fell silent. It made sense. Brian's secretary, his frequent absences, the many women at his funeral . . . so that was why Luisa cried and why Vittorio had been upset to know of her tears. If only she'd known! Luisa had shielded her from the knowledge. It was clear why Vittorio hated Brian and herself so much. Brian had stolen the woman he loved, deceived her cruelly and assuaged his guilt with presents. One of which was instrumental in her death. How he must hate them!

She drew her hands from Rico's and covered her face, sobbing weakly, keening over her blindness about her brother's character. He'd had no guidance, she told herself. He'd been given wealth and not the strength to deal with it.

'Please, please don't cry,' begged Rico. 'You're not to blame.'

She sobbed on. He sighed and brought her head to rest on his shoulder, patting her back gently till she had cried herself out.

'I'm not sorry I told you, though I've gone against Vittorio's wishes. He tried to save you from pain and not tell you of Brian's infidelity. He thought you had been hurt enough to know of the gambling. You're better now?'

Vittorio had been *considerate?* She bit her lip. Why hadn't he shown his hatred for her family by telling her the whole truth? Why should he want to protect her?

'I'm OK,' she said, with a wan smile. Rico looked so anxious and had been so kind that she took his face between her hands and kissed him tenderly on each cheek, then rose gracefully and they walked back, arms around each other's waist, in a new understanding. Neither of them noticed the man who had walked to his bedroom window to let in a little air, and who had seen the kiss, the exchanged looks and the attentive way Rico bent over Jemma's blonde head.

It was fortunate that they did not see him. For the violence on his face would have petrified them both.

CHAPTER SEVEN

HURRYING along the landing shortly after dawn the next morning, Jemma found that in her haste not to be late she had forgotten her watch. Rising early was something she hadn't yet become accustomed to. She returned to her room and located it on a chest in the bathroom.

A sound alerted her and, thinking it was the maid, she called out in Italian as she tried to fix the awkward catch on the strap.

'Anna? Is that you? Can you come and help me with this?'

'No, it's me, Rico. Are you having difficulty with something? Can I help?'

She went to the bathroom door, still fumbling with her watch, and saw Rico hovering uncertainly in the corridor.

'Hello,' she smiled. 'I won't be a moment. I'm just trying to—oh, bother!'

'Those little clasps can be so annoying. *Permesso,*' he said gallantly, striding over.

'Thank you,' she smiled, holding up her wrist. Rico bent his golden head to see how the catch worked and deftly snapped it into place, playing the gallant by kissing her inner wrist. But Jemma was frozen in horror at the sight of Vittorio who stood on the landing, watching in white-lipped shock as Rico placed his hand lightly in the small of her back, ready to escort her downstairs.

She couldn't move for the paralysing effect of the fury on Vittorio's face, and she knew what this must look like.

He must be thinking history repeats itself, she thought bleakly.

Rico was, by now, aware of the anger that lashed from his brother's glittering hard eyes.

'Vivi, please, this . . .'

'Breakfast is ready and so am I, Jemma,' said Vittorio harshly, striding away.

His body looked as taut as a bow-string. Jemma knew she'd have to wait for a suitable moment and explain what had happened, or he'd take it on himself to warn Rico off. He'd almost certainly tell Rico his version of the scene with Dave and blacken her character, and she didn't want to lose Rico as a friend. She needed every one she could make, she thought gloomily.

'Madonna!'

'Oh, Rico, we didn't do anything wrong. I'll talk to him later. Leave it to me. For the moment, if he wants to make a fool of himself, then that's his problem. I won't be cowed by him.'

'Such courage! But I don't want him to think badly of us. A man of such honour, who commands our love and respect, is deeply hurt when he thinks his relatives have fallen below his own standards.'

Poor Rico. He didn't know about Vittorio's Casanova tactics abroad, or the way he was treating her. She couldn't disillusion him—Vittorio would do that one day.

'This house seems to revolve around Vittorio de Vasari,' she said sharply, 'and I'm fed up with it. Besides, he must have been in the same situation himself plenty of times. He can hardly criticise.'

'Vivi?' Rico shrugged. 'There are many stories. But his life is discreet. We know nothing of his intimate friendships. He is popular, yes, but no scandal has ever touched him.'

'That's only because he hasn't been caught,' she said tartly.

A loud bellow from downstairs reached them and Rico flinched. 'You are going down?' he asked nervously.

'Of course I am.'

'You will suffer his temper.'

'Words can hardly do much to me,' she said with a shrug.

'You are as bold as my mother. But you are right, he won't hurt you physically; after all, you are a guest in his home. But I . . .'

'Rico, I hate the sight of blood,' grinned Jemma. 'Why don't you stay away from him till he comes back, and save me that nasty experience?'

'I can't leave you to face him alone.'

'I'd rather you did. I must go; if I'm late he'll have something else to complain about. Go on, Rico, I can handle him.'

'I really think you can,' he said in admiration. 'He has a terrible temper, beware. When he loses control, there is no knowing what he will do. Vittorio's passion runs high, like Father's.'

'He can't hurt me, I tell you,' she said with a certainty she didn't really feel. 'You really should stay away. Sorry I caused this trouble.'

'Sweet Jemma,' he smiled ruefully. 'You and Vittorio will always be trouble together.'

He was right, she thought with resignation. Being within five miles of each other seemed to bring a series of disasters and problems! It was going to be difficult, convincing Vittorio that she wasn't in the process of seducing Rico in order to marry him. For Rico's sake, she'd have to try.

The ingrained manners of a lifetime prevailed when Jemma entered the breakfast room, causing Vittorio to rise very briefly from his seat and resume it without looking at her. With a sharp snap of his newspaper, he lifted it between them as a barrier while Jemma munched through three croissants. Little of him could be seen; an outstretched foot, an ankle encased in dark green trousers, the cuff of his green and white-striped shirt. But she could *feel* the controlled violence, the seething brain, preparing scathing words of condemnation. This time, she wouldn't let him get away with jumping to conclusions.

It was five to seven. Slowly the paper was folded and placed on the table. His head was lowered, his gaze on the coffee-cup he was picking up, and then his head lifted, his gaze crawling slowly over Jemma's delicate white lawn shirtwaister, the cinched belt, the trim bodice, the area of pale gold skin at her throat, and then he raised eyes of loathing to her face.

Oh, God! she thought. He looks like a rampaging bull!

Keeping his eyes on her, he tossed down the last of his coffee.

'I hope you've not exhausted yourself. I need you to be alert this morning,' he growled.

'Do I look exhausted?' she asked calmly, knowing that was the only way to stop him from exploding.

His lashes flickered over her with slow insolence. 'No. You look revitalised. I like a woman with stamina,' he said throatily.

'Don't be insulting,' she snapped.

'I wouldn't dream of insulting a lady,' he countered, with a snarl to his lips. 'You're different.'

Forgetting her intention to cool the situation, Jemma rose to his bait. 'You hate to think that I might prefer someone else to you, don't you?' she cried recklessly.

'My God! You slut! Did Rico spend the night with you?' he yelled, the wild flame of temper thrusting him to his feet.

It was her turn to let her scornful eyes flash up and down his body. 'I won't even consider answering such a stupid, disgusting question,' she shot back.

'You'll keep your claws off Rico,' he breathed, his chest heaving in suppressed fury.

'He was only——'

'*Off! Do you hear?*' he yelled.

Jemma bridled. 'You think so little of your brother——'

'*Gesù!*'

Then she was hit by a whirlwind as he stormed around the table and almost launched himself at her, turning her around in her antique gilt chair and tilting it back against the table, his hot breath heating her face, his own quite distorted in manic rage. 'You will not let him touch you, do you hear?' he spat. 'He is not to hold your hand, kiss your lips, caress your body, or even get within *reach* of you! *Do . . . you . . . understand?*'

Frightened though she was, Jemma was also incensed at his high-handedness. Once again he'd believed the worst of her, and all the time she was innocent. He was the most pig-headed man she'd ever known, the most arrogant . . . Well, there was only one way to deal with tempers. He deserved to sweat. Rico was in no danger at the moment, and she'd clear up the situation during the day. For now, she'd hurt Vittorio as much as he'd hurt her by his lack of trust. More than anything she'd wanted that; without trust, there could be no love.

So her eyes challenged his, she smiled mysteriously and slowly removed a speck of pastry from the corner of her mouth with a slick of her tongue.

'Hell!' he rasped. 'Don't push me,' he said with slow menace.

'I wouldn't dream of it,' she said languidly. 'I'd have to touch you. Well, *are* you jealous?'

It was obviously the ultimate insult, to suggest that he might be interested in her. His nostrils pinched inwards as his eyes glittered balefully. 'Too far,' he spat. 'Even for a woman who acts like she lives in the Travestere. If you understand my meaning.'

'It's the ghetto district, in Rome,' she said calmly, examining a perfect fingernail. 'I believe there are whores there, though I don't have your personal knowledge of their charms.'

His roar deafened her. He'd let the chair drop back on its fragile legs and was lifting her and shaking her by the shoulders till her head whirled and all the pins in her hair shot out, so that her thick, milky tresses fell over her eyes.

A cruel hand gripped the back of her neck, forcing her to meet his gaze. His pupils were huge and black, his mouth a terrifying snarl, and his sheer physical strength weakened her resolve to withstand him.

'I will teach you that I am not to played with,' he grated. 'There will be atonement for your sins. Some of your debt will be paid today, at length. You have driven me to the edge and beyond. God knows I've tried not to be tempted by you! But every minute of the day you look at me out of your innocent baby-blue eyes, crossing and uncrossing those slender legs, lifting that beautiful ribcage and taunting me with your siren's body!'

His hand slid down to her knee and she gasped as it slithered upwards over her smooth thigh. She jerked back, but the hand at her nape snapped her forwards again.

'And you sway your hips enticingly,' he said huskily, running a hot palm down to her waist and around her hip-bone. 'And your breasts,' he crooned, his eyes heavily lidded and sultry now, as his fingers delicately brushed each rising curve.

Jemma was weak with longing. She fought to keep her eyes open but they insisted on fluttering, and all she was aware of was a wash of heat that encompassed them both.

'God!' he groaned.

She felt his mouth touching hers and sank into his arms. The kiss was gentle and sweet, tormentingly so, as if he didn't dare to give in to the violent, carnal feelings evidently within. For Jemma felt him shuddering as he kissed her. She *had* gone too far, she thought, wishing she could give in completely to this indolent pleasure that threatened to swamp her.

Imprisoned in the circle of his arms, she felt a growing desire to respond. Her body was doing enough of that for itself, as it was, with the tight bloom of her breasts stretching the thin material of her dress. Vittorio had discovered this, too. Jemma jerked at the exquisite sensation as his thumb gently rubbed across one hard, aching peak.

'Please don't,' she moaned.

'I can't help myself,' he said hoarsely. 'I need this.'

A sharp kick of desire burned into Jemma, and her involuntary gasp made his eyes gleam avidly. The fever spread through her body even as his searching, sensual mouth plundered hers, his hands moving on her breasts in the slow, steady rhythm of a practised seducer. Jemma summoned up her weakening resolve as she felt his fingers slide up her thigh.

In desperation, she sank her teeth into his lip—not hard enough to provoke his wrath, just enough to tell him she was still fighting. To her dismay, he gave a low, husky laugh and drew her lip between his teeth, too. She had never known such an intensely erotic sensation as his tongue caressed the swollen lip, the naked desire in his eyes riveting her to the spot.

Then those eyes narrowed. Into her consciousness came a clacking sound from the marble hall outside, and Vittorio suddenly released Jemma with a harsh exhalation of breath, striding like a dangerous animal to his chair just as his mother walked into the room.

'Such a dreadful roaring noise I could hear just now. We must check the water pipes,' said the Marchesa with suspicious innocence.

'Morning, Mother,' he growled.

Jemma surreptitiously tried to restore order to her hair as he bent urbanely over the Marchesa's hand, blocking her view.

'Dearest. I have an early breakfast because there is much to do. I am going to see . . .' She stopped, disconcerted by Jemma's dishevelled appearance, and frowned. 'Morning, Jemma.' Her eyebrow arched. 'A little early for that, Vivi?' she murmured.

Jemma blushed scarlet. 'You don't understand,' she said shakily, holding on to the table. 'I was late. Please excuse my untidiness. You know how punctual I have to be.' It was all true, she thought.

'There! Your bullying brings Jemma down looking as if you'd been making love to her all night,' said the Marchesa, making Jemma gulp at her frankness. 'He works you hard, but he is a good teacher. He will teach you many things.'

She didn't dare to look at Vittorio. What he wanted to teach her was the kind of lesson she didn't dare to begin.

As far as he was concerned, it was now a matter of personal pride, the macho factor, that she should succumb. The fact that she had apparently given her favours to practically everyone else must infuriate him! How far would he go? That violence just now had made her believe he might force her. Certainly no one would believe that the gentlemanly *Conte* would ever stoop to such behaviour. He could get away with almost anything and remain unpunished. She remembered the triple-parked car in Rome and shivered.

'Cold, Jemma?' he muttered, glaring at her from under his lashes.

'No.'

The Marchesa looked shrewdly from one to the other and smiled. 'Jemma looks hot to me. Almost as hot as you do.' They both stared at her, knowing she was well aware that they had been arguing fiercely. 'Vivi, you don't seem to be in the right mood for me to ask this, but you'll be leaving soon and I must because I forgot to yesterday. I'd like you to bring Jemma back early. The Mayor of Montevecchio has asked us to tea.'

Vittorio's brows drew together. 'Thank him for the invitation and give our regrets.'

'You must come!'

'We have things to do.' He looked impatiently at his watch. Jemma had never heard him speak so sharply to his mother before. 'We're late. No, there's no time for you to do your hair, Jemma. We have to leave now.'

'But, Vittorio,' coaxed the Marchesa, 'wouldn't you like the Mayor's daughter to meet Jemma?'

Mother and son locked eyes, he proud and angry, she not expecting that he would refuse her request. The Mayor's daughter was obviously prize bait.

'Maybe. I promise nothing, since you didn't warn me,' he said tightly, bowed, and walked to the door. 'Come, Jemma!'

'Foolish boy,' murmured his mother. 'He wants you all to himself.'

Jemma stumbled blindly, then recovered. He wanted to have her. He wouldn't particularly care how or where, as long as he did.

Numbly she walked to the door and then stopped. She didn't have to go. She could wait until . . . Vittorio grabbed her elbow, his momentum carrying them along and the power of his body as he manhandled her into the car filling her with sickening fear.

She reached for the door, but it had been locked automatically.

'Let me out!' she shouted.

He didn't answer, but gunned the engine, and Jemma smelt burning rubber as they made an impossibly tight turn and the car roared like an angry lion down the long drive.

'You may think this is a game, Jemma, but it isn't. We have work to do. You must learn, learn, learn! And we must get rid of you as soon as possible. Now, the work I set you . . .'

He began to fire questions at her, trying to find out whether she'd learnt the complex laws he'd told her to study the previous night. Jemma had spent some time trying to fix in her mind the difference between the different Registers and Habitation documents, but his manner was so intimidating that she had a mental block.

'I can't remember,' she said coldly for the umpteenth time.

'You don't remember?' he sneered. 'Either you have

suddenly developed a dreadful memory, or you didn't bother to work at all last night. Too busy entertaining my brother, I suppose. Too eager to discover what there is to know about the Visconte Enrico Francesco de Vasari to do what you're paid for!'

'What I'm *not* paid for!' she snapped.

'Out.'

They'd stopped by a lovely lake, a small paved area on one side of them bright with tables and striped sunshades, and a modern development of flats on the other.

'Or do you want me to touch you?' he murmured.

'Open the door,' she croaked.

He released the door, his arm trapping her. 'Number six,' he muttered. 'Don't be long or I'll come and get you.'

That lent wings to her heels. She took the keys from him and slid her legs out, wishing he didn't eye them so lasciviously. It didn't help her pulse-rate.

'Not bad,' he said, glancing through her notes when she returned. 'You deserve a reward.'

Jemma thrust herself back as his arms moved around her, but it was useless. She stiffened, her face becoming frigid.

'You'll like it,' he murmured. 'I only wish you didn't. It would please me more.'

'If it entails being touched by you, I'll probably be violently ill,' she breathed.

He laughed cynically and there came that deep, slow kiss again, making her gasp with its sensuality, and she felt herself going under. His mouth gently coaxed hers open and, totally against her will, she allowed him access to its moist interior.

'Beautiful, beautiful,' he whispered, savouring her sweetness.

And the hot, heady taste of him set her on fire. His fingers ran wildly through her hair and caught it in a knot, making her more his prisoner. His mouth travelled down to her throat, caressing her skin with his lips, then slow, languorous sensations rocked her as his tongue flickered and snaked its way around the hollows. Vittorio groaned deep in his throat, and Jemma felt the harsh and incredibly erotic tug of his teeth on her flesh.

'Good, good,' he muttered, snapping the seat-belt around her and driving away, leaving some shocked and startled tourists in the pavement café.

'Don't do that again!' she grated, wiping her hand across her mouth.

'Again and again and again,' he said harshly.

Next time they stopped, thought Jemma, she'd look around for someone to help. She'd scream and make a fuss so that he was embarrassed. Being treated like this was soul-destroying, and she hated him for what he was doing.

Gone was the gentle beauty in his face that she had admired. Instead there brooded a devil, intent on bending her to his will. Nothing but bitterness shaped his mouth, and his nostrils flared in a haughty sneer. To him she was dirt, and he could therefore do whatever he liked to her without a twinge of conscience.

Jemma nervously took in his powerful frame and knew that resisting him would be impossible. All she could hope for was that he'd make her take details of a property near human habitation before he attempted to assault her again, and she could summon help.

'About last night——' she began.

'I don't want to hear!' he breathed.

'You must. Rico——'

'Damn you!'

The car began to slow down on a deserted stretch of road and she felt sick with nerves. With a squeal of brakes, he stopped and reached for her again.

'No,' she moaned.

'Yes,' he said, his eyes glittering febrilely. 'I want to drive all thoughts of Rico from your mind. I want you. I want to touch you. Over and over again. I can't keep my hands away from your body.'

As she struggled he reached inside her shirtwaister, and the feel of his fingers on the soft, rising flesh above her lacy bra completely destroyed Jemma's defences. 'Vittorio . . .'

'Yes. It *is* good between us, isn't it? Here,' he muttered. 'Undo my shirt. Touch *me,* Jemma!'

'Please, no . . .' How *could* she want him? How could she be fooled by his gently murmuring words, his hot eyes and lightly stroking fingers? He was tearing his shirt open, then his fingers stripped down her buttons to open the front of her dress completely, snatching at her belt and allowing himself access to her breasts. Her protests were ignored. His eyes lighted on the front fastening of her bra, and suddenly her breasts were tumbling eagerly into his hands and he was making soft, guttural noises in his throat as she mindlessly gripped his shoulders. She had to stop him.

His long index finger stretched out and lightly touched the rosy peak of her breast just as she flattened her trembling, protesting hands against the hard planes of his chest. They both gasped with the dual sensations.

'Jemma,' he muttered, 'I can't get enough of you. Respond to me.'

'I won't,' she said through clenched teeth.

Each ruby-red crest hardened and lengthened under his

delicate touch. He brought his thumb into play, squeezing and releasing, driving her wild as the pains speared fast and furious to her loins.

'Vittorio, don't do this to me,' she husked.

'It's your fault. You've provoked me for long enough.' His head swooped to suckle at her breast, his lashes lying thickly on his cheeks. 'Do you like that, mmm? Does that excite you?'

'No! Stop,' she moaned, yearning and aching for more. Her fingers found the vulnerable muscle in his shoulders and dug in, all her weight pushing behind them.

'Patience,' he muttered, flinching away. 'I have a better way to use your angry energy. And you are angry, aren't you, Jemma?' he said throatily.

'Yes!' she groaned.

'Good. So am I. And more aroused than I have ever been in my life. I think this is going to be an enjoyable day.'

He leaned back a little, his uneven, rasping breath sending shivers down Jemma's spine every time it feathered her throat.

She winced. 'My God! I hate you!' she breathed. Wearily, she tried to draw her dress together. 'Does it go on for much longer, this punishment?' she asked in a dead tone.

'That depends on you.'

'If you're waiting for me to beg you to make love to me, then you'll have a long wait.' She watched his fingers fumbling with his shirt-buttons, hardly able to fasten them. 'Is this what you planned from the start?' she asked, her eyes electric-blue in her intense emotion.

'No!' he snarled.

'I don't believe you! You set out to spoil my life because Brian spoiled Luisa's with his infidelity!'

'You *have* been getting cosy with Rico, haven't you, for him to tell you that? He must think a lot of you to defy me and risk my displeasure. I'm sorry you know. It isn't pleasant to be disillusioned about people you love.'

She winced at his bitterness, thinking that there were no illusions left for her now. 'Why did you bring me to Italy?' she asked in a low voice.

'I told you, my mother. She complained day and night till I relented and agreed to help you and give you a chance to stand on your own feet. I realise now that it was a mistake—you're nothing but trouble. I never thought I'd want to touch you, but I was wrong.'

'I'll tear you to pieces before I let you maul me around again!'

'Really?' he drawled. 'I think we will fight a little and then your natural urges will overcome you. Now, one more house and we stop for lunch.'

Jemma stared at him in amazement. 'I'm not going anywhere with you!' she rasped. 'I've had enough of this.'

'Then you must prepare for a jail sentence,' he said implacably. 'I think, Jemma, I have you in my power.'

'You're *evil!*' she breathed. 'Does it please you to know that the only way you can keep me here is by blackmail?'

Her wrist was caught by his steel-tight fingers. 'You stay because you want something,' he growled. 'If not me, then you'll settle for Rico. I give you fair warning, Jemma, however much I hate myself for treating you as I have, if you try to seduce him, I'll lay you down and take you so fast that you won't even have time to cry out.' His eyes were locked with hers in fierce combat. Jemma sensed the explosive fury within him and despaired.

'What are we having for lunch?' she asked coolly, shaking inside.

Vittorio laughed. 'Jemma,' he grinned, 'I look forward to taking you. And, unlike the rest of your lovers, you won't find that you can control me, or that you will easily forget my lovemaking!'

Still laughing to himself, he snapped on his seat-belt. There was little Jemma could do. All she had were her wits and her ability to remain cold and detached. But for how long?

Her nerves in shreds, they drove into wild, untamed countryside, over a rough country road. The property was old, an abandoned farm, very rambling, with the usual animal rooms on the ground floor, wine and olive presses, and simple rooms above. It would need a great deal of renovation, but the floors were all in terracotta, the tiled roof was sound and the land supported olives and vines and a pear and cherry orchard.

Inwardly seething, Jemma took details to Vittorio's strict rules, and because she refused to speak to him he soon wandered off in boredom. Finished at last, she waited miserably by the old well, leaning against its warm stones. In the drowsy heat, lizards basked in the sun close to her feet, and larks soared overhead. One bird, high up, so high that it was only a speck, suddenly dived like a stone into the orchard.

'What are you dreaming about, Jemma?'

Vittorio's big, warm hands turned her around, and rested lightly on her waist.

'Nothing,' she said, pulling away in panic. This was to be his seduction scene, she thought, her mouth going dry.

Then she saw the rug on the ground beneath a huge chestnut tree and realised he was intending they should eat here.

She glanced at her watch. 'It's only a quarter to one,'

she said sarcastically. 'We have fifteen minutes of working time left.'

'You are going to work,' he said lazily, arranging his long length on the rug and patting the space beside him. 'Come, sit down and I will tell you some things you need to know.'

Jemma tried to concentrate on what he was saying about arranging bargain flight offers and viewing packs, and bent her head, taking copious notes, while his voice grew steadily lower, huskier and more sexy by the minute. Her fingers were shaking so much that she could hardly write.

'Now it is one o'clock,' he said, mockingly. 'Time to eat.'

And drink, it seemed. He'd brought a bottle of red wine—'full-bodied', as he described it, with a slick of his tongue over his lips that sent quivers of delight into Jemma's tense nerves. She refused to drink much, but the wine was potent in combination with the midday heat. Her tension increased as she slowly and reluctantly finished the last grape, and drained the last drop in her glass, which was etched, she noticed hazily, with his damn lions rampant!

'Next,' he murmured, while her heart hammered away, 'we rest.'

In unbelievable relief, Jemma watched him lie back with his hands behind his head and close his thick lashes over his eyes. The rituals had to be observed, it seemed, even when seduction was in the air. First lunch, then a siesta, *then* make advances. So much for passionate Italians!

The wine had made her sleepy, too, and they had been up since dawn. A rest was sensible, but she was damned if she'd let herself sleep. She couldn't tear her eyes from his face. Relaxed, it lost some of its daunting haughtiness and pride. The high, princely cheekbones still carved strong ridges that gave way to the dark hollows of his cheeks, where Jemma longed to place her mouth, and his nose was arrogantly Roman. But now that his hard, mocking eyes were covered by the dark fringe of lashes he seemed more approachable and vulnerable, especially, she thought, his mouth. It was drawing her closer with its cresting curves, the cynical lines smoothed away in repose.

With a shock, she saw that he was watching her sleepily, no scorn in those blue eyes that echoed the sky, only . . . She felt her lips tremble and part at his invitation.

'Come here,' he said softly.

She shook her head and her mouth shaped in a silent 'No!'

He reached out a friendly arm, and she shook her head again. 'You're angry that I am sleepy?' he murmured. 'You want me to make love to you now?'

At the shock in her eyes, he laughed in delight, reaching up and deftly pulling her on top of him, so that she was unable to move.

'Such an eager woman,' he whispered in her ear, his warm breath sensitising her nerves and arousing her further. 'I have slept so badly over the past few nights, Jemma, and all because of you. Now you are here, and willing, I am drowsy. That's ironic, is it not?'

'I'm not willing . . .'

'Ever since I knew you were coming here, I have been driving everyone mad,' he murmured, sliding her to lie beside him in his arms. He lifted himself slightly and looked down on her, his eyes warm and full of passion. Jemma felt the familiar feeling of pained, unfulfilled loving biting deeply and averted her head in anguish.

'I have worked non-stop ever since the funeral and I

am exhausted,' he said. 'It was my reaction to you that made Mother nervous. She knew how much it mattered to me whether you liked her or not.'

Jemma tried to understand what he was saying, but her brain was fuddled from the warmth, the wine and his golden voice. There was just one thing she wanted: him. And his heart had been given to his dead cousin.

'But now I have you in my arms,' he murmured, 'I find that I am not sleepy, after all. It's a miracle what a woman's body can do to a man, yes?'

'I—I wish you'd leave me alone,' she said miserably.

'How can I? I am human, a man, with a man's desires and passions.' His fingers tormented her lips and she jerked her head away in irritation. 'I like to be teased, Jemma,' he said, with a note of steel in his voice, 'but not for ever. Don't you miss it all? So long without a man touching you . . .'

'If you don't get your hands off me, I will complain to your mother,' she spat, her eyes ablaze with dark fury. 'She'll take my side, I'm sure.'

'Maybe. Why don't you find out? I'll take you home now.' When she stayed put, staring at him, his mouth twisted wryly. 'You *don't* want to go home? Can you want me to seduce you, then?'

Jemma jumped to her feet like lightning, his laughter following her as she ran back through a field of white marguerites, the aching emptiness of her loins taunting her.

He was risking a lot, she thought bitterly, suggesting she could tell his mother everything. She wouldn't, she couldn't hurt the Marchesa by exposing her son's cruel vendetta, and Vittorio had sensed that. Only if he harassed her seriously would she go to the Marchesa for help.

'Working out what you'll say? How you will prove I've

been molesting you?' he asked with a smile, when he joined her in the car.

'That's right,' she said calmly.

'How cool you are! Will you be so cool when I explain that I felt at liberty to treat you like a whore because you are one? After I've told my mother everything, she couldn't help but realise you are fair game, especially if Rico is made to speak of your betrayal of my hospitality.'

'You call your dictatorial, feudal behaviour hospitality? Sure you weren't related to the Borgias?'

'Only distantly,' he drawled. 'Jemma, if you decide to talk to my mother, please do it after tea.'

'I'd forgotten! I can't go . . .'

'You will,' he said grimly, 'if I have to tie you up and carry you there in a sack.'

'That'll make a novel entrance,' she said coolly.

Vittorio's sharply expelled breath told her that he was annoyed at her lack of fear. It was a successful defence, it seemed.

When they drew up to the *palazzo*, he told her she could spend the next few hours doing her hair and her nails in preparation for tea.

'Be in the hall at ten to six and we will all walk in together. It is impolite to be late.'

'It's a long time till then. I think I'll do some sightseeing,' she said.

'No. You will not. There is no one to go with you. Stay in the *palazzo* grounds.'

Jemma jutted out her chin and said no more, planning to have a swim in the pool and then take the little Fiat for a drive. It would be marvellous to escape from his overpowering presence.

In fact she was unable to swim, because he'd reached

the pool first. She watched from the wrought-iron gate as he surged relentlessly up and down, no doubt swimming off his frustration. Well, there was no way that she was going to get into the same pool, even in her very proper one-piece suit. Annoyed, she went back and changed, even more determined to escape for a brief break before meeting the Mayor.

It did seem like running away from jail, to be out of his reach for a while! She'd found the keys of the Fiat in the ignition, so hadn't bothered to ask permission, knowing she was unlikely to get it. Everyone seemed to be out or taking a siesta still. Happily she drove through the archway, the gates opening by remote control from the car, and down the corkscrew road into the countryside.

It was very hot. She stopped to open all the windows and slide back the sun-roof. To her left she spotted a minor road leading into uninhabited countryside, and she decided to take this so that she could be quite alone with her thoughts. The road began to rise up a large hill, obviously owned by someone wealthy, for notices all around told her that the area was reserved for boar-hunting. She negotiated the narrow hairpin bends, trying not to look at the drop to one side, where the road was level with the tops of trees.

As she rounded a tight bend, her eardrums were blasted by two deafening explosions that seemed to rocket a few inches over the open roof of the car. She screamed, swerved, saw she was heading for the sheer drop, screamed again and jammed on the brakes as she wrenched the steering wheel around.

Silence. Jemma could feel her whole body shaking. The car had stopped within a foot or so of the edge. A small movement made her look to her left: a stocky man had risen from the bushes and he was holding a shotgun which was pointing straight at her. He wore breeches, boots and a military-type jacket with epaulettes, and a bandolier was slung around his shoulders. A crazy gunman!

White-hot rage erupted inside her and, without stopping to think, she flew out of the car like an avenging fury. She stormed up to him and snatched the weapon boldly out of his hands while he stared at her in astonishment. Too wildly angry to speak Italian, she yelled at him hysterically, waving the gun, screaming at him that he'd almost killed her, that he was an idiot for shooting downwards and across a road, that he must have heard the car coming, that only a mindless child would bang away at anything that moved without safety checks first, and that she'd report him to every authority she could find in the telephone book.

In the midst of this attack, several heads slowly rose from the bushes behind the man, watching her in stunned disbelief. She didn't care, she was too terrified and too *mad* to take any notice. To emphasise the danger she'd been in, she pointed the gun at him threateningly and he took several nervous steps backwards. Then she dropped it contemptuously on the ground and stamped up and down on it to release the irrational feelings that consumed her.

Only then did she turn on her heel and get into the car, driving away, her knees trembling dreadfully and her hands so clammy on the steering wheel that she could hardly maintain her grip. Once clear of the area, and in a flat river valley, she stopped and sat still, just shaking and staring ahead in numb shock.

Gradually she became aware of the sound of a powerful engine in the distance. As it became throatier, she heaved a sigh of relief. Unbelievably, Vittorio had found her. How he had done so she didn't know and didn't particularly care. She needed his big chest and strong shoulders to lean on.

A glance in the mirror confirmed that it was Vittorio, driving like a madman. He screeched to a stop beside the Fiat and leapt out, wrenching open her door before she could move.

'You fool!' he yelled. 'I told you not to go out on your own!'

'I—I—Vittorio——'

'How can you be so irresponsible? If you're going to act like this, as thoughtlessly as your brother, then I'll have to seriously reconsider appointing you as my manager.'

Jemma's eyes blazed. 'You *dare* renege on your promise! I wasn't to know that men here are gun-crazy kids!' she yelled back. 'I've nearly been killed! I could have been blown apart by a shotgun or gone off the road and ended up being burnt alive!'

'What did you say?' he breathed, his face white. 'Explain.'

She passed a shaking hand over her face. 'I can't. I don't want to talk about it. I was petrified. Petrified!'

'You'd better,' he said tightly. 'That was the Mayor of Montevecchio you pointed a gun at. It was the Mayor's gun you stamped on, the Mayor you humiliated in front of all his friends.'

'I don't care, he deserved it! Besides, how do you know all this? How did you know where to find me?' she demanded.

'When I was told you'd taken the car, I only had to ask. You're very conspicuous, and everyone around here knows my Fiat. I know what time you crossed the road to Gubbio, that you waved at a man on a donkey near San

Nicolo, and that you insulted the Mayor while he was shooting wild boar.'

'And me! Don't I have any privacy at all?' she yelled.

'Many eyes watch over women, it's the custom,' he snapped. 'Now tell me what happened.'

'Why don't you get your spies to tell you?'

'Damn you, Jemma! I'm asking you! Will you tell me or do I have to shake you?'

'I'm sick to death of you macho men,' she spat. 'I'm afraid,' she continued with heavy irony, 'that I was stupid enough to drive along a public road and not know that around a bend a gun-toting Mayor was intending to shoot the roof off the Fiat. Or perhaps he was aiming at my head . . .'

'Wait! He said nothing of this . . .'

'I bet he didn't!' she yelled, beside herself with anger. 'Why should he admit to you that he nearly shot me and that I almost drove off the road in terror?'

His expletive shocked her into startled silence. Vittorio never swore like that!

He shook his head, evidently angry with himself. 'I'm sorry,' he said tightly. 'When I was told the direction you took, when the Mayor . . . My *God!* I will kill the bastard! I will . . .'

'Vittorio! No!' she cried, horrified at the primeval light in his eyes and the vicious twist to his mouth. 'It's enough that I've made him a laughing stock. Please do nothing!'

'I must,' he muttered, then gazed down on her with perplexed eyes. 'Oh, Jemma,' he said softly. 'You bring so many of my emotions to the surface. I am so uncontrolled . . . To think that you might have been killed . . .' His voice cracked and her mouth opened in astonishment. 'Don't look at me like that,' he breathed. 'For God's sake,

Jemma, I can't stand it!'

'Like . . . what?' she asked, unnerved to find how husky her voice was.

Then he was hauling her out of the car and kissing her, not gently or sweetly, but wildly, totally unrestrained, as though he was ensuring that his lips were for ever imprinted on hers, whatever should happen to them in the future. Crushed in his arms, her back arched against the tiny car, she was powerless to stop him as his mouth drove harshly into hers. It seemed he needed to blot out some memory and to relieve the frustration that had built up during the day.

Shuddering, she raised weakened arms and slowly drew her fingers through his sun-gold hair.

'Gently, Vittorio,' she said softly.

'I can't, I can't!' he groaned. 'You don't know . . . You must never disobey me like that again, do you hear?' he murmured thickly, his thumb tracing the line of her heavily swelling upper lip.

In her loving heart, she imagined that he cared, and a storm of feeling threatened to overwhelm her. He shifted to warn her of his arousal, and she looked up with dazed eyes as he ran his fingers along the line of her hip-bone, then splayed his hands over her buttocks, caressing their gentle swell. His mouth nuzzled her throat and his breath fell sweetly on her face.

The blood roared in her head and her pulses danced so fast that she wondered how her body could withstand such pressures as he groaned and eased away. She couldn't stand this any more. She needed him too much.

Vittorio stroked her hair and held her to him tightly before drawing back.

'Wrong place, sweetheart,' he said quietly. 'I have

somewhere special in mind.'

'Not the Three Bears' cottage?' she laughed lightly, trying to find some control.

He smiled and shook his head. 'A little more upmarket,' he murmured.

'Oh, the Wolf's pad,' she joked, successfully concealing her nervousness.

'Right. Shall we go?'

Jemma swallowed. He looked dangerous, atavistic, totally male, and she felt suddenly afraid now that they weren't even touching. 'I——'

'Why do you torment me like this?' he whispered, fingering her mouth.

'I can't trust you,' said Jemma. 'I don't know if this is part of your revenge, or if you really want me. And if you do, I'm not sure how you'll treat me. One moment you're all softness and the next you're foul; I never know where I am with you!'

'Then I think it's time I showed you . . .'

'No,' she said quietly. 'Vittorio, I was so pleased to see you just now, to think that I had someone to turn to, but all you did was shout at me——'

'I was——'

'I know,' she interrupted, 'you were angry that I'd been disobedient. Well, I'm a grown woman, not a child; I don't want your protection, I don't want your suffocating attempts at domination. I want my freedom. You're punishing me for something that Brian did, and you must see that it's unfair. Stop trying to hurt me. You've succeeded. You've made my life miserable. Now leave me alone.'

She made to open the Fiat's door, but he was too quick for her. He removed the keys and put them in his pocket.

CHAPTER EIGHT

'I WILL drive you back,' said Vittorio impassively. 'You'll accompany me to Montevecchio, be charming to the Mayor, and then I'll make arrangements to send you home.'

'Oh, yes?' scorned Jemma. 'Thanks, but I'd rather walk than fall for that one. All you want to do is get me in the car so you can assault me.'

'No,' he said in an oddly cracked voice. 'You think I like what I am doing? Look at me and see that I'm telling the truth. *Look*, Jemma!'

Her set, white face turned towards him reluctantly and she steeled herself for the desire that would flow from his eyes. Yet something strange had happened to him: there was no desire, only despair. It seemed that he'd recognised at last that she wasn't going to give in.

'I can't take any more,' he said huskily. 'Your debts are paid. Go back to England and work beside my manager; learn the job and start a new life.'

'Home? You're sending me home?' she blurted out. This was what she'd wanted, to be free of him, and now it had come to that, all she could think of was that she'd never see him again. Never taste his lips, never laugh with him, tease him . . . 'Ohhhh . . .' she moaned, whirling around to hide her face, her quivering mouth, trembling hands and the tears that threatened to blind her.

'Jemma?' he said uncertainly.

She'd been stupid! If she'd allowed him to make love to

her, he would have kept her here until he looked for more variety, and she would have had *something* of him to take back. As it was, she left emptied of everything, even sexual fulfilment.

She loved him that much, she thought in wonder. Loved him more than her pride, her idiotic morality, her inner cry for *his* love.

'Jemma!' came his harsh voice.

Her head shook from side to side, refusing to turn. Then, although she couldn't see because of the tears rolling silently down her cheeks, she knew he was walking around to face her and she swung away. In vain: his breath fanned her face and he could see the final breakdown of her defence.

'Why? Why are you crying?' he asked sharply.

For a long time he pestered her, refusing to accept her shaking head as an answer, and by now her tears were flowing freely and great sobs were wrenched from her body.

'Answer me! Why are you upset? I *must* know!'

'Be-be-cause . . . I . . . *love* you . . . you bastard!' she yelled eventually.

Stupefied, he made no move towards her, just stood motionless while she mopped her eyes, readying herself for the scorn that would be poured on her head.

'How long have you loved me?' he asked tightly.

'Ages!' she shot at him defiantly. 'And I hope that makes you feel good! I fell for you when we first met, and it's been like riding a bucking bronco ever since!'

'You've hated me, fought me . . .'

'You turned your back on me!' she yelled. 'You chose to misjudge me without asking for an explanation.'

'Gesù! What did you expect? You were in bed, in the dark, panting and flushed, with a man lying across you,

fondling your breasts! What the hell do you expect me to believe? In fairies? That Santa Claus is alive and well? That you were doing it in your sleep?'

Jemma covered her ears. 'Stop it, stop it!'

'When I ran upstairs to find you, eager to tell you I had returned, I passed so many couples strewn everywhere that Ancient Rome would have snapped them up for their orgies!' he shouted.

'Well it was nothing to do with me!' she cried, infuriated. 'I was trying to sleep. Dave barged in and began mauling me. He was *dressed*, Vittorio. Didn't you notice? And he had his hand over my mouth, trying to stop me from yelling for help. Surely you noticed *that?*'

'Don't shout at me!' he yelled. 'I can shout louder and faster! And if you expect me to believe that . . .'

'No,' she said, suddenly quiet. 'I gave up all hope of you trusting me, long ago. But it's true, Vittorio. Every word.'

He was silent. Then he passed a shaky hand over his forehead. 'I—I saw you, I . . .' He met her honest, unhappy eyes and the colour drained from his face. 'You didn't explain . . . you could have run after me——'

'What was the point?' she asked wearily. 'You'd made it quite clear what you thought of me and Brian. I was so hurt. Brian said that you didn't really care about me. That was obvious when you believed the worst without hearing my side of it.'

'Brian,' he breathed harshly.

'Yes. *He* cared enough about me to put me straight about you. And when I heard how you tried to come between him and Luisa, I was glad that I hadn't become involved with such a small-minded autocrat,' she said bitterly.

'Oh, my God!' muttered Vittorio. 'And you love me . . .

now?'

She lifted her head proudly. 'Now, God help me,' she said quietly. He could do whatever he liked: laugh, taunt her, send her home—nothing mattered any more.

'Get in the car.'

Weary and resigned, she obeyed, sensing how tense he was. His face was set in grim lines and his knuckles were white from gripping the steering wheel so tightly. The car gently throbbed into life and slowly moved away. Tiredness washed over her. It had been a long, long day. The thrum of the engine dulled her brain. Losing her bearings, she frowned at the sight of a hill town bristling with tall towers against the Tuscan skyline. They must be near San Gimigniano—and far from the *palazzo.*

'Where are you taking me? The Mayor . . .'

'To hell with the Mayor,' growled Vittorio.

'No, please,' she cried, her mouth dry with fear.

'All these years,' he said in a monotone, 'I wanted to hurt you with a savage intensity that threw me off balance. It grew inside me, Jemma, till I could no longer enjoy women. You did that to me. I had never known such an intense hunger. I was almost emasculated. Sex for its own sake relieves nothing in the end. And so I am hungry. Very, very hungry. And we are going to do something about that, right now. Tea, I think, will not be enough for what I have in mind.'

'Vittorio . . .' Jemma could hardly breathe. Her hands fluttered nervously in her lap. There was a still certainty about him. And a dangerous sexual arousal. Where was he going? She'd longed to belong to him, but not this way, not in anger. His possession would be brutal, a travesty of the love she bore him.

'The way you flirted with me,' he rasped. 'You

practically invited me to jump into bed with you, when you were just a young woman. Remember? You were so bold, and I warned you that I was a full-blooded man and not to be treated lightly. But you wanted that, didn't you? You knew what I was telling you and welcomed it. You were eager for sex and I couldn't resist your siren call.'

'No, it wasn't like that,' she said hoarsely. 'You were going to leave and hadn't kissed me. I wanted you to kiss me!'

He grinned wolfishly and Jemma cringed. He didn't believe her—he really thought she'd known what she was doing. Her fingers twisted in her lap frantically. Vittorio stamped on the accelerator and her heart was in her mouth as they swung around the bends in the road. Between them, the air seemed hung with wires, strung to a high tension. They both sat with rigid spines, keyed-up with suspense, waiting for the inevitable climax. But who would win? Jemma asked herself.

Outside, even the air was unusually oppressive. It had become very hot, with the electricity-charged atmosphere of a summer storm that was brewing, its dark purple clouds lowering over the distant hills. In the distance was a gentle rumble of thunder, which set the stage for Vittorio's final act of revenge. In the heavily laden air, Jemma's head began to throb until she had to close her eyes in pain.

'Oh, the penalties of a night of love,' he mocked harshly. 'Finding the lack of sleep is getting to you?'

She ignored him.

'Poor Jemma. Perhaps I drove you to finding release.'

A gentle finger trailed down her cheek and she drew away sharply. 'How heavily you're breathing,' he murmured, and Jemma's eyes shot open as his hand lightly caressed the curve of her breast. 'Do you find my touch exciting?'

'About as exciting as watching paint dry,' she said laconically, hoping to unnerve him.

Vittorio laughed menacingly. 'You're trying to incite me,' he said, his voice husky. 'Sometimes I wonder whether you know how provocative you are, whether you are intentionally driving me to the edge.'

His eyes gleamed and Jemma was frightened by their intensity. They had driven into San Gimigniano now, through a stark and gloomy gate, and along a medieval street, quite deserted because of the impending thunderstorm. Into the skyline soared the tall, brooding towers, black and almost windowless against the leaden sky. They looked as menacing as the harsh man beside her.

The sky was turning a deep purple. Jemma noticed that the car was nearly going slowly enough for her to open the door and roll out. She bit her lip, took a deep breath, and then her eyes widened in terror as Vittorio drove straight towards one of the towers. For a split second she thought they were going to crash into the heavy wooden doors, then they swung open to allow the car inside. The doors dropped down again, leaving them in darkness, and Jemma knew she was trapped.

Vittorio reached over and hauled her towards him, with Jemma fighting all the way. He laughed softly and drew her out.

'What are you doing?' she yelled stupidly.

'Taking you!' he growled. 'I've waited years for this.'

Gone was the suave, elegant and courteous Count. This was a man with no mercy, a man on the edge of control, with but one thing in mind. Her fists beat on his chest but made no impression, and she was lifted effortlessly and carried through an archway, up wooden spiral stairs, on

and on, yet he never paused, the ferocity of his anger and
unrelenting desire driving him upwards.

'Hush, *amore*,' he commanded. 'Give in to your love.'

Jemma winced and continued to plead hoarsely. They
had reached the top of the two-hundred-foot tower. No
one would hear her cries.

'Gently,' he muttered. 'Don't exhaust yourself.'

He kicked open a door and it slammed behind them.
Jemma only had a moment to register that the windows
looked out on to the valley far below, that there were
frescos on the walls and vaulted ceilings, and then her
despairing gaze took in the huge silk-canopied bed,
covered in white furs. Then Vittorio was sliding her feet to
the ground, down the length of his body, the movement
rucking up her skirt, and his hands were everywhere, his
lips crushing hers, his breathing harsh.

'I want you,' he muttered. 'I am going to have you. And
show you what loving can be like.'

Her nerves quivered and coiled. This was the real man, a
predatory animal of unleashed sexuality, using his steel
strength to get whatever he wanted.

'Don't do this, please, not like this,' she moaned.

'I have no choice. I am driven: that's my misfortune,'
he husked. 'You've taunted me beyond my patience. Now
I teach you, once and for all.'

His hands stilled, cupping her face as he opened her
mouth with his, telling her with his tongue what was to
happen to her. She felt herself going under, being swept
away in the tide of loving need, sorrowing for his
desperation, wishing with all her heart that she could
evoke love in him and tame his wildness.

'Jemma!' He threw his head back and she was filled
with the urge to ravish the long, brown length of his

neck, to feel the powerful panther shoulders under her fingers again.'Want me, want me!'

The savagery of his voice brought a trembling to her body, knowing that what he asked was already true. Tormented, she moaned as his hand cradled her swelling breast beneath the dress and almost reverently traced its shape, while his sweet lips trembled over hers.

'God! You're irresistible! No wonder other men flocked to your bed! You've left me with no pride, that I should want you, too!'

'No, Vittorio!' she denied.

'I never thought it would happen to me,' he growled. 'Never imagined that I could desire a woman of easy virtue. My honour and self-respect is in shreds! If only you didn't love me . . .'

He spread his hands over her bottom and pulled her hard into his body. Jemma felt stabs of pain to see him looking so magnificent, with his eyes glowing and his proud head lifted as if in agony. His vengeance would be bitter-sweet for both of them. His knee thrust between her legs and she could take no more.

The wild craving exploded inside her, and she felt him tense in shock as she shuddered and cried aloud for him. Then she was being thrown on to the bed, deep into the furs, and it seemed he couldn't get enough of her, was fired with a terrible hunger that had them both tearing at his zip, and then his hands were roughly stripping away her briefs.

The silken fur erotically caressed her body and Jemma writhed in helpless delight. She wanted him. She begged, pleaded, stretched out her arms as he quickly removed his own briefs, closing her eyes momentarily at the sight of his virility. Impatiently he straddled her.

'Jemma.' It was hardly a word. He was as frenzied as she. 'God! I . . . can't . . .'

There came a hot, savagely scorching thrust that filled her with pain, and she arched right off the bed in shock, feeling him pause, and the violent throb of his body. She cried out for him to love her, and with quick, fierce thrusts he drove deeper and deeper, till her head thrashed wildly on the bed and her body moved like a slender reed beneath his hands, sliding, arching, bucking to his demand. She clutched his arms, dazedly watching the primitive passions on his face, until she was aware of nothing else but the shattering, body-cramping explosion that crashed in wave after wave through every inch of her, and all the long hungry years were washed away in the splendour of their lovemaking.

She lay panting beneath his hard-muscled body that was bathed in a film of moisture. He was clenching at the fur with a desperate fist, perspiration beading his forehead, his eyes tightly shut. Her pulses still beat wildly, but she was replete. Nothing but that violence would have satisfied her; it had needed that, to relieve the frustrated anger that had grown between them. It had been perfect. Yet she felt shame, now, at the pagan creature she had become in his arms. Or was this how it was for everyone? She listened to his unsteady breathing and shuddered to think of his certain contempt.

'Jemma.'

Her name was like a whispering breeze. Summoning up all her strength, she opened her eyes lazily and forced herself to speak. 'You might think you've won, but you haven't. Because you've given me something I'll always remember.'

In those moments of passion, her mind had so deceived

her that she could imagine they were in love. For a short while she'd known what it must be like for married lovers, and she could always keep that in her heart.

'And you gave me something that was very important to you. I ought to beat you,' he growled.

'Oh. That bad?' she quavered.

The fist tightened and he was poised above her, his face suffused with fury. 'Jemma, Jemma, Jemma . . . You . . . I . . . *Madonna!* The one time in my life—*my life*—that I treat a woman like that . . . I act like a wild animal . . . and it has to be you! *And* you are not the experienced woman I thought, but a virgin!'

'Oh.'

'Is that all you have to say? I half rape you and . . . With a willing, experienced woman, maybe it would have been . . . Jemma! What of all the men I imagined! The men you implied you'd loved? Rico? Why the hell didn't you tell me? Didn't you think it would make a difference? Look at your body! Look at mine! What have I done? What have you done to me?'

emma tried to understand his anger, but the sight of the red nail marks on his body disconcerted her. She'd done that without even knowing. 'There were no men,' she whispered. 'No men at all. Especially Rico. It was all innocent.'

'Oh, *hell!*' he groaned, covering his eyes. 'Can you imagine how I felt, wanting you so much and half believing that my own brother . . . Have you any idea how much I loathed myself?'

'I tried to tell you, but you wouldn't listen,' she cried.

'It changes everything. I've been such an idiot. You see, when we drove up from Rome, you woke from your sleep and called to a lover.' He hovered over her, his eyes dark with pain. 'That's when I decided for certain that you weren't innocent—and you confirmed that!'

'I called to *you!*' Would he never stop tormenting her and probing, finding out how deeply she loved him?

He buried his head in her shoulder and began to nuzzle it, murmuring indistinctly. Jemma flinched as a great roll of thunder filled the room, and lightning crackled like a pistol shot, flooding them with its neon glare. She flung herself deep into the bed, trying to draw the white fur over her for protection. Vittorio's arms gathered her up, and then she was safe and secure against his warm, golden chest.

'Don't be afraid,' he murmured in her ear.

'Afraid? I fear so much: the storm, you . . .'

'Why be afraid of me? Gently, gently, *amore*,' he crooned as a flash illuminated the room again.

She bit her lip. Please don't be nice to me, she cried silently. Be passionate, possess me, but don't make me like you! Parting would be more painful.

'Tell me,' he coaxed, his finger teasing her breast.

'You'll hurt me,' she whispered.

'Oh, God!' he groaned. 'Forgive me! I won't hurt you again. Let me touch you.' His hands moved to her thighs, but she protested. 'I'll show you how gentle I can be, I promise,' he murmured throatily.

'I don't mean physically hurt, I mean mentally. When you——' she gulped, and he turned her chin up so that she was forced to look at him. 'When you leave me,' she finished miserably.

'You want me to stay in bed with you *all* the time?' he grinned.

'Damn you, Vittorio, you know what I mean! *Oh!*'

The tower shook with thunder. Rooks rose screaming

from their nesting places in the ancient walls and took flight
with raucous calls. Jemma buried her head in Vittorio's
chest while his hands and velvet voice calmed her.

'We're safe here.'

'I'd be safer with . . .'

'Wild donkeys?' he teased, laughing when she flushed.
'This tower has stood for six hundred years. Why should it
collapse today, when we are making love?'

'There were seventy-nine towers once,' she muttered.
'And only thirteen left now.'

'They fell from war and neglect, not storms. Anyway,
do you imagine that lightning would dare to strike
anything owned by *Il Conte* Vittorio Romano de Vasari di
Montevecchio?'

'It belongs to you?'

He brushed her lips tenderly, holding her as she flinched
at the startling, sizzling light again. 'Look at the walls.
They are my ancestors, painted by Gozzoli. Do you
recognise likenesses of me?'

She was so astonished that she ignored the thunder and
sat up, under the red, pleated canopy. The paintings
depicted wedding scenes—scenes *after* the wedding, in the
bridal suite, earthy, amorous, erotic . . .

She fought down an urge to turn away, and kept her dry
lips together when she badly wanted to slick her tongue
over them. She knew he was watching her intently and
would see that as an invititation.

Her lashes finally lowered to shut out the image of a
handsome, naked man pleasuring a golden-haired
Renaissance princess. He looked just like Vittorio. Sharp
pains seared her body.

'He was a merchant prince,' Vittorio smiled. 'He traded
furs with Russia. His mouth is like mine, yes? And the

bride——' His voice lowered to a throaty growl. 'She is nearly as beautiful as you.'

Down the centuries, the reality and intensity of the scenes rang out as true and as lifelike as if she was watching herself with Vittorio in a huge mirror.

'Hardly anyone knows of this treasure. Only one woman has ever entered my ivory tower,' he murmured.

Misery surged through Jemma. She knew who that was. Luisa.

'And now you are here.' He looked down on her. 'We were in such a hurry to make love that we only removed the essentials,' he grinned. 'But now we'll take away the rest of the barriers. I'm hungry again, and this time it will be long and slow and gentle. And very, very tormenting.'

But she was cold and he stared, puzzled, at her icy look and rigid body. 'What have I said? What's the matter?' he asked.

'You would actually bring me to your . . . wolf's lair, where you've already made love to Luisa?' she breathed.

'No, of course I haven't . . .'

'You *bastard*! You *liar*! How can I believe anything you say now? You loved her, I know you did.'

'Of course!'

'And you expect me to believe that you brought her here and played cards or something? I know how sensual you are, remember, and I've heard of the way you can't leave women alone. London has never been the same since you left!'

'What are you talking about?' he asked, suddenly grim.

'Brian told me about your tom-catting, he was with you,' she said. 'You taught him how to sink to your level.'

'It's as well that your brother isn't alive, Jemma, or I'd half kill him,' he growled. 'That's the trouble with someone who lives a lie, he didn't know when to stop—when his interfering would be harmful. Listen to this, and while you're listening, look into your heart and then into mine. God knows I've tried to shield you from your brother's weak character, but this time our future is at stake. First, I was working too hard to spend any time with women in London. In fact, ever since I left you in that thug's arms, I've done little else but work. Often through the night. I've loved you from the moment I first kissed you. Work was the only way to cope with rampant insomnia and violent jealousy.' He smiled wryly.

Love! Jemma couldn't believe her ears. He couldn't mean it. 'But why should Brian say you were a rake?' she said doubtfully.

'Maybe he wanted to give you a reason to get over me,' he suggested.

Jemma frowned, remembering. 'I was crying. He wanted me to stop—you see, he hated me to be weak. Oh, God! He lied for my sake!'

'I think so. I didn't bring Luisa here, only my mother. Jemma, you've seen how I adore my family, my aunts, cousins, the little children. I'm a very affectionate man, haven't you noticed?' His lips brushed hers and her eyes, awash with tears, tried to focus. He kissed each one to help, and savoured the salt tears with his tongue. 'I loved Luisa. But it's *nothing* to what I feel for you. God, haven't you felt its power? That it's driven me to smash every idea of honour I ever cherished? That on the day I saw my beloved cousin buried, I looked at you, dishevelled and seductive, and felt shaming desire and love? Hell, if that maid hadn't left the door open, I would have taken you then and there!'

'Oh!'

'Yes, oh. It would have saved a lot of trouble, too,' he added grimly. 'I could have been making love to you in all those damn properties we tramped through.'

He was waiting: waiting to know if she believed him, and there was no doubting the way he looked at her. None at all. She remembered their closeness on the days when they'd had fun, his joy, the happiness he gave to others and the overwhelming feelings that captured her every time he smiled at her. Suddenly she had the courage to believe that this man could love her. She raised huge, melting eyes.

'*Madonna!* I love you. Once I told you I wanted everything. I still do. Be prepared for total commitment. Marriage, twenty-seven children——'

Jemma giggled. 'Isn't that rather a lot?' she demurred.

He hugged her to him. 'Not really. We need to start a new dynasty to rid the woods of woman-eating donkeys.'

She pulled away in mock anger, leaning over him in a threatening posture. 'You'll never let me forget that, will you?' she complained.

'I could, every now and then,' he suggested. His eyes lazily contemplated her breasts and her breathing quickened. Slowly she bent her body and gently swayed till each one in turn swept across his lips.

'Now,' she encouraged softly as his mouth responded. 'Help me to pay my debt.'

'There's a lot to pay,' he mumbled, his mouth full of her rosy peak. 'It could take years and years and years.'

'I know. I'm looking forward to each instalment.'

'*Madonna!*' he whispered, kissing her forehead, her eyes, her lips. From the window, a pure golden shaft of light touched their bodies, and they exchanged smiles at the omen. 'I'm glad we found our love here, Jemma. This tower will always hold special memories. When we're married, I'll abduct you often and carry you here. Yes? You'd like that?'

He had been kissing her throat, and his voice was becoming huskier. Jemma feathered her fingers over his wave-cut mouth, and a fierce bolt of desire stirred within her. 'I want you,' she said with all the boldness of a woman in love.

'You shall have me, my darling,' he growled. 'Gently, slowly, sweetly and with love. Then, perhaps, with urgency, as you become more daring and torment me more. Again and again till you are weak and trembling and sure of my adoration.'

Jemma gave a shiver of pure anticipation. 'You have a lot to live up to,' she said softly, indicating his amorous ancestor.

'Hmmm, so I have,' he said, the flowing liquid of his voice filling her senses. He bent to trail kisses over her scented shoulders. 'A matter of honour.' His eyes looked at her with tenderness. 'Shall we begin to make our own thunder and lightning? Our own electricity?'

Jemma gasped as Vittorio began to arouse storms within her, the love in his eyes filled her with a wild, exuberant joy. His ancestors looked on with envy and satisfaction, knowing that this union would last for ever.

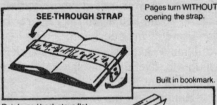

"GIVE YOUR HEART TO HARLEQUIN" SWEEPSTAKES

OFFICIAL RULES

NO PURCHASE NECESSARY TO ENTER OR RECEIVE A PRIZE

1. To enter and join the Harlequin Reader Service, rub off the concealment device on all game tickets. This will reveal the values for each Sweepstakes entry number and the number of free books you will receive. Accepting the free books will automatically entitle you to also receive a free bonus gift. If you do not wish to take advantage of our introduction to the Harlequin Reader Service but wish to enter the Sweepstakes only, rub off the concealment device on tickets #1-3 only. To enter, return your entire sheet of tickets. Incomplete and/or inaccurate entries are not eligible for that section or sections of prizes. Not responsible for mutilated or unreadable entries or inadvertent printing errors. Mechanically reproduced entries are null and void.

2. Either way, your Sweepstakes numbers will be compared against the list of winning numbers generated at random by computer. In the event that all prizes are not claimed, random drawings will be held from all entries received from all presentations to award all unclaimed prizes. All cash prizes are payable in U.S. funds. This is in addition to any free, surprise or mystery gifts that might be offered. The following prizes are awarded in this sweepstakes:

(1)	*Grand Prize	$1,000,000	Annuity
(1)	First Prize	$35,000	
(1)	Second Prize	$10,000	
(3)	Third Prize	$5,000	
(10)	Fourth Prize	$1,000	
(25)	Fifth Prize	$500	
(5000)	Sixth Prize	$5	

   *The Grand Prize is payable through a $1,000,000 annuity. Winner may elect to receive $25,000 a year for 40 years, totaling up to $1,000,000 without interest, or $350,000 in one cash payment. Winners selected will receive the prizes offered in the Sweepstakes promotion they receive.
   Entrants may cancel the Reader Service at any time without cost or obligation to buy (see details in center insert card).

3. Versions of this Sweepstakes with different graphics may appear in other mailings or at retail outlets by Torstar Corp. and its affiliates. This promotion is being conducted under the supervision of Marden-Kane, Inc., an independent judging organization. By entering the Sweepstakes, each entrant accepts and agrees to be bound by these rules and the decisions of the judges, which shall be final and binding. Odds of winning are dependent upon the total number of entries received. Taxes, if any, are the sole responsibility of the winners. Prizes are nontransferable. All entries must be received by March 31, 1990. The drawing will take place on April 30, 1990, at the offices of Marden-Kane, Inc., Lake Success, N.Y.

4. This offer is open to residents of the U.S., Great Britain and Canada, 18 years or older, except employees of Torstar Corp., its affiliates, and subsidiaries, Marden-Kane, Inc. and all other agencies and persons connected with conducting this Sweepstakes. All federal, state and local laws apply. Void wherever prohibited or restricted by law.

5. Winners will be notified by mail and may be required to execute an affidavit of eligibility and release that must be returned within 14 days after notification. Canadian winners will be required to answer a skill-testing question. Winners consent to the use of their name, photograph and/or likeness for advertising and publicity in conjunction with this and similar promotions without additional compensation. One prize per family or household.

6. For a list of our most current major prizewinners, send a stamped, self-addressed envelope to: WINNERS LIST, c/o MARDEN-KANE, INC., P.O. BOX 701, SAYREVILLE, N.J. 08872

LTY-H49